RED

BY

SUSAN L. PARE'

RED   Susan L. Paré

Red- All contents copyright © 2019 Susan L. Pare.

All rights reserved.

Printed in the United States of America.

First Edition: Red - February 2019

All rights reserved.

Cover designed by Susan L. Pare'

ISBN-13: 978-1-7335572-0-7

RED   Susan L. Paré

MORE BOOKS BY THIS AUTHOR

The House on Ludington Street

What's Behind the Screen Door?

The Mayor's Son

Willerton Woods

Cowtown

Floating Face Down
A Sheriff "Cowboy" Berkson Mystery Novel – Book Three

Let's Play Autopsy

A Bad Week in Hollister
A Sheriff "Cowboy" Berkson Mystery Novel – Book Two

Don't Smother Your Mother
A Sheriff "Cowboy" Berkson Mystery Novel – Book One

Crossing Sydney

Blueberries and Bears and My Brother's Shoes
First Edition – out of print

Contents

<u>May, 2017</u>

RED   Susan L. Paré

One

"Grams, are you okay?"

"Of course, I'm okay. Why wouldn't I be okay?" Tillie replied as she picked herself up off the sidewalk.

"You just fell down, that's why," Lynn said, trying not to laugh.

"I didn't fall down. I tripped." Her grandmother looked over at her and frowned. "Do you think this is funny? I could have killed myself, you know."

"No, Grams, I don't think that fall would have killed you. You could have broken a hip, though. This is the second time you've fallen this week. You really need to be more careful."

"I'm always careful. And, it's the third time, not the second."

"Well, if this is the third time when was the second time?"

Tillie gave her a blank stare. "That can't be right. Maybe, it's the fourth time. No, it's definitely the third one. Oh, what difference does it make, anyway? I never seem to hurt myself. It's just that these damn sidewalks are. . . Oh, my!"

"What's the matter?"

"See here? My knee is bleeding. I guess that must have happened when I tripped over the sidewalk."

"You think?" Lynn bent down and checked her grandmother's knee. "You scraped it pretty bad." She reached into her jeans pocket, pulled out some tissue, and held it against her grandmother's injury.

"I hope that tissue hasn't been used," Tillie

commented.

"Of course, it hasn't," Lynn replied.

"You're pushing kind of hard, dear."

"I'm sorry, but the pressure will help stop the bleeding. I think we better go back to the house."

"No. I'll be all right in a minute. Just push on it a little longer."

"Sorry, Grams. We need to clean that knee and put a bandage on it. Let's go."

Her grandmother didn't move.

"Are you coming?" Lynn asked.

"I don't think I can walk with this bad knee," she replied.

"Well, I can't carry you, so what do you suggest we do now," Lynn asked, holding back a smile.

"The house isn't that far. Why don't you go get the car?"

"I'm not getting the car. I think you can make it okay. Come on," Lynn said, taking her grandmother's arm.

Tillie pulled her arm away. "I don't think so. You should go back to the house and get me a chair, so I can sit here and rest a while," she said, smiling sweetly.

Lynn put her hands on her hips and stared at her grandmother.

"What?" her grandmother asked innocently.

"You can't honestly believe I'd fall for that again, do you."

Her grandmother looked confused. "Fall for what, dear?

"You know what. The last time this happened, it

took us two hours to find you. It's not going to happen again, old lady. At least, it isn't on my watch."

Tillie sighed. "I just wanted to take a little walk around the block."

"That's not going to happen now, so let's go back to the house."

Her grandmother shot her a dirty look. "You can be a real pain in the ass, Lynn."

"You need a walker. Why doesn't mom get you a walker with those wheels that help steady you?"

"Don't even start with me. I'm not now and never will be one of those old farts using wheels."

"Then, how about a cane? A cane would be good. There are some super fancy ones that you can buy."

Tillie just shook her head. "You and your mother are going to be the death of me. Let me tell you one more time, Lynn. I'm not using a cane or a walker or a wheelchair. Got it?"

Lynn reached out and took Tillie's arm. "We'll see."

The two women started to slowly walk back to Tillie's house. Suddenly, the old woman pulled her arm away and looked her granddaughter in the eyes. "I've got it!" she exclaimed.

"Well, I don't want it, so don't give it to me," Lynn replied, grinning.

"Aren't you the funny little thing?" her grandma said, sarcastically. "Seriously, Lynn, I've got the solution." She hesitated, thinking about what she was going to say.

Lynn waited. "Just what are you talking about?" Lynn finally asked her.

"Is my driver's license still good?"

Lynn looked puzzled. "Why do you want to know that?"

"Is it or isn't it?" Tillie asked sternly.

"I don't know, Grams, but I seriously doubt it."

"I have to go check it out." She grabbed her granddaughter's arm and pulled. "Come on. Let's get going."

Lynn stayed put. "What are you up to?"

Tillie let loose of her granddaughter's arm. "I've decided to get one of those things that you can ride around on."

Lynn closed her eyes and took a deep breath. "Please tell me that you don't mean a mobility scooter."

"I guess that's what they're called. That's why I have to check my driver's license. To see if it's still good, so I can drive one of those. Tillie took Lynn's arm again and started walking toward the house. "If my license has expired, will you take me to get a new one?"

"We'll see."

"I think I want a red one. Or, blue. What do you like better, Lynn? Red or blue?"

"Oh, that's up to you. After all, you'll be the one riding it."

Tillie thought for a moment. "Red," she uttered.

"Grams?" Lynn said after they had walked a few dozen steps.

"Yes, dear?"

"When we get back to the house and you check out your driver's license, I think you should check out the balance in your checking account, too."

Tillie stopped in the middle of the sidewalk and looked at her granddaughter. "Why would I do that?"

"I'm sorry to give you bad news, but those scooters cost around $3,000.00. I don't think you have that kind of money. Or, do you have a stash hidden away that we don't know about?"

Tillie grinned. "Do you think I don't know that they're expensive? I can read, you know."

"I know. It's just that you don't have that kind of money and I doubt that mom and dad are going to pay for it. I'm sorry, but I guess you're out of luck.

"I read a lot, you know. I read about these scooters all the time."

"Of course, you do. Come on, let's get in the house and take care of your knee."

Tillie took Lynn's arm and continued walking towards the house. "Of course," she said, "I don't think I'll need a license if I don't drive my scooter on the street."

Lynn rolled her eyes. "You're not getting a scooter. You can't afford one."

Tillie laughed. "Of course, I'm getting one. All I need is for my doctor to write a note and . . ."

Lynn waited. "And, what?" she finally asked.

"Medicare will pay for it," Tillie said, with a smug look on her face.

"What?" Lynn stopped dead in her tracks. "No way!" she exclaimed.

"Ta-da," Tillie sang out with a laugh, as she spread out her arms and stuck her left foot out in front of her, striking a pose.

"Mom?" Lynn called out, as soon as they were in

the house. "Grams hurt herself again. Get in here."

"What did she do now?" Rosemary, Lynn's mom, said with a sigh as she walked into the living room.

"She fell on the sidewalk and hurt her knee. I kept telling her to pick up her feet or. . ."

"I didn't fall," Tillie said, defensively. "It's those damn sidewalks that aren't even. I tripped, that's all."

Lynn looked at her mom. "Sorry. I meant to say that she tripped," she said, hoping to pacify her grandmother.

"That's right. I tripped," her grandmother agreed.

"And, then she fell," Lynn added, grinning.

Rosemary glared at her daughter. "You just can't leave well enough alone, can you?"

"Sorry, I couldn't help myself," Lynn told her, smiling.

"Let me see it," Rosemary said, as she bent down to look at her mother's knee. "You did a good job this time, Mother. That must really hurt," she declared.

"I hardly feel it," Tillie told her.

"Well, it looks like it would hurt a lot. Lynn, we'll need the extra-large gauze bandages."

"I'm on it," Lynn replied, as she headed for the bathroom.

"And, bring some of that antiseptic with you. We need to clean all the dirt off before we bandage it."

"Which antiseptic?" Lynn asked her.

"The red one."

Tillie gave her daughter a dirty look and plumped herself down in a chair. "Really, Rosemary? The red one?"

"It's the best one," Rosemary told her mother.

6

"Bullshit! It's the one that hurts the most and you know it."

"Lynn?" Rosemary called out.

"What?"

"Bring the other one. Your grandmother thinks I'm trying to hurt her."

Lynn walked into the living room and handed her mother the bandages and a bottle of antiseptic.

"That's the red one," Tillie said. "Get the other one."

"Guess what, mom?" Lynn said. "Grams has been talking about buying an electric scooter."

Rosemary looked up at Lynn. "What brought that on?" she asked, a miserable look on her face.

"I mentioned that she should get a walker."

"I told you I'm not getting a walker. I'm getting a scooter," Tillie said, emphatically.

Rosemary took some gauze, poured a little of the red antiseptic on it, and started to clean the dirt off of her mother's knee.

"That hurts," Tillie cried out.

"I'm sorry, but I need to make sure it's clean."

"I'm getting a red one," Millie commented.

Rosemary looked up at her daughter, who was grinning. "I'm so glad you see the humor in this," she said.

"I need to get going. Is there anything you need before I leave?" Lynn asked her mother.

"I thought you were going to stay for dinner," Rosemary said.

"Lynn said I should get the red one, didn't you Lynn?"

"Did you Lynn? Did you tell your grandmother she should get a red scooter?" Rosemary asked her daughter.

"Really, mother? Of course not."

"Do you think I should see a doctor about my knee?" Tillie asked, smiling.

"Your knee is going to be just fine, Mother," Rosemary said.

"Lynn, will you take me to see the doctor?"

"No. You just want to see your doctor so she will write you a note to give to Medicare, so you can get a scooter."

"Enough talk about this. You are not getting a scooter," Rosemary stated.

"Yes, I am," Tillie retorted.

"Over my dead body," Rosemary said. She finished taping the wound and stood up. "There, that should take care of it."

"I know people, you know. I could have you wiped out just like that," Tillie told her, snapping her fingers.

Lynn bent down and kissed her grandmother on the cheek. "Love you. Bye. See you Sunday, Mom."

"Are you going to leave me alone with her?" Rosemary asked her daughter.

Lynn gave her mother a big smile and waved goodbye, as she left the house.

Two

Sunday lunch was the highlight of the week for Rosemary. Since her father had passed away four years ago and she and her husband had moved in to care for her mother, it had become a family tradition. Rosemary expected her family to be there every Sunday. Joseph, her husband, expected them to be there, too. And, on time.

Lynn was rushing. She had slept late and by the time she showered and decided what to wear, she was running at least a half-hour behind schedule. Her father was a strict but usually pleasant enough man. He did not, however, appreciate having to wait for his lunch because one of his children couldn't make the weekly event on time. So, at one o'clock sharp, unless the house had blown away due to a tornado, earthquake, or flood, lunch was served. If you arrived late to the table, you were chastised in front of the entire family and you didn't get dessert.

Of course, this didn't mean a whole lot, seeing the Larson children had heard their father's rantings all their lives. Unless that is, you had brought a guest. Then, you and your guest would be totally embarrassed by Joseph, Sr., while everyone's food got cold, as he went on and on and on.

Lynn grinned, as she thought about the last time she had arrived late to lunch at her parent's home. She had brought Jason, her flavor of the month, along that day, which had been a huge mistake now that she thought about it. It took all of her willpower to not break out into laughter, as her father read her the

9

riot act. However, when he started to lecture Jason about the virtues of being on time, everything went south. Jason, a forty-year-old man, was not about to put up with being yelled at by a stranger. He had simply stood up and walked out of the front door without so much as a 'by your leave'.

This had left Lynn stranded at her parent's house without her car, which meant begging Junior for a ride home. He finally agreed to drive her, but only after she gave him a twenty to help pay for the gas.

The Larson children, Lynn, Stacy, and Joseph, Jr., did their best to arrive on time, but crap can happen and this was one of those Sundays when it most certainly was about to hit the fan.

Lynn looked around the room to be sure she had turned everything off. She double-checked the coffee pot, saw the red light shining bright, grabbed her purse, and ran out the door, already dreading the upcoming meal.

Lynn pulled out of her driveway and took off practically burning rubber. She was seriously late. She considered turning around and going back home. She could call and say she was sick or something. However, as she well knew, trying to remember a lie can wear you out, and you just wind up getting in more trouble. So, she put her foot down on the gas and began her drive to Columbus, so she could spend a few hours with her family.

Joseph Larson, Sr. looked up at the grandfather's clock, then, checked his watch. It was almost twelve-thirty and none of his children had arrived. He was tired of these Sunday family get-togethers. They had been going on for years, and he wished he could just eat his lunch in peace and quiet, watch some sports on TV, take a nap, and tune out the world.

However, Rosemary enjoyed seeing her children at least once a week, so he kept quiet. Taking care of his mother-in-law was no easy task, his wife didn't ask for much, and he figured it was the most he could do for her.

But, one of these days. . . Well, he'd toss the idea of cutting back to every other week into the air and see where it landed.

Hearing a car door slam, he looked out the front window and saw Stacy getting out of her car. Well, at least one of my children is on time today, he thought to himself.

"You're late," her father yelled, as she walked through the door."

"Hi. Sorry about that, Dad." Lynn looked at the dining room table and saw that two of the seats were empty. Her brother wasn't there. "Looks like I'm not the only one that's late," she declared. "Where's Junior?"

"He isn't coming," her mother told her. "He just called. He's sick."

"Really? What's his problem?" Lynn asked her mother.

"Probably Sunday flu," Stacy said. "I almost came down with it myself."

Lynn grinned. "I fought it all the way here." She

sat down at the table and reached for the potatoes. "Must be going around."

"Lynn, you must learn to allocate your time better. You arrive later and later every Sunday and it's very upsetting," her father said, beginning his lecture on timeliness.

"I know, Dad. I said I was sorry." She looked over at Stacy, who was sitting across from her. "Where are Simon and the kids?" she asked.

"David had a game," Stacy told her sister.

"So, where's Lele?"

"Lisa had a sleepover. I'm picking her up after I leave here. And, I wish you wouldn't call her that."

"You realize that you don't get desert today, don't you?" her father continued.

"Yes, Dad, I know."

"I'll send some home with you," Rosemary said.

"No!" her father yelled. "She doesn't get to take dessert home. If she can't be here on time, she doesn't get dessert. Not here and not to take home. Never!"

"I'm getting a scooter," Tillie said quietly. "It's gonna be a red one."

Everyone at the table looked at Tillie. "I'm getting a note from my doctor," she added.

Joseph, Sr., looking confused, glanced across the table at his wife. "What the hell is she talking about?"

"Nothing. Just forget it," Rosemary told him.

Stacy looked at Lynn and grinned.

"Stop it," Lynn mouthed, trying not to laugh.

"May I please be excused?" Lynn asked her

mother, twenty minutes later.

"Of course, dear," Rosemary said, smiling at her youngest daughter.

As Lynn started to get up from the table, her father put his fork down on his dessert plate and stared at her.

"What?" she asked him.

"You know the rules, Lynn. You may leave the table when we are all done eating."

"Well, I'm done and mother said I could be excused. Anyway, why should I have to sit here and watch everyone eat dessert when I don't get any?" she asked him, knowing she had just opened a can of worms with her flippant remark.

"And, whose fault is that," her father asked her, as he shoved a huge forkful of cake into his mouth.

Lynn sat back in her chair and stared at her father while he finished his cake. He's going to ask for another piece, she thought to herself. And, he'll drag out eating it as long as he can, just to aggravate me.

"Mother," Joseph said to his wife, "I could sure go for another piece of that cake." He picked up his plate and held it out to her.

And, there it is, Lynn thought, getting irritated. "Let's not do this anymore," Lynn said loudly and stood up. "I'm sick of these Sunday meals. Once in a while is fine, but why should I come here every Sunday, just to be insulted and treated like a little kid? I'm thirty-three years old, for crying out loud. And, I'm sick of it."

Rosemary gasped.

"I'm sorry, mother, but it's true. Look at father.

It's obvious he hates these family meals, too. So, he entertains himself by making us all miserable." She looked at her father, whose face was turning red with anger. "Isn't that right, dad? You hate them as much as I do, don't you?"

Suddenly, her father slapped his left arm and cried out.

"Joseph? Are you okay?" Rosemary yelled. "What's wrong? Stacy, do something."

"I think he's having a heart attack," Lynn told her mother. She glanced over at Stacy and yelled, "Call 911."

"It might be a stroke," Stacy said. "His mouth looks like it's drooping."

"I'm on it," Tillie cried out, as she pulled her cell phone out of her pocket.

"Put that damn phone away, Tillie," Joseph shouted. "Something stung me." He reached down and picked a dead wasp up off of the floor. "It's a damn wasp." He threw the wasp on Lynn's plate. "Here's your dessert. Have your mother wrap that up for you to take home."

"Joseph," Rosemary yelled. "What is wrong with you?"

"They're on their way," Tillie said, as she glanced up from her phone and looked at Joseph. "Oh," she uttered, "he looks all right now. I don't think he had a heart attack after all."

"Yes, Mother, Joseph is fine," Rosemary said. "He was stung by a wasp and lost his mind for a moment. That's all."

"Well, that is a relief," Tillie said. "After all, if

something happens to him, who's going to help me put my new scooter together?"

"I think I hear sirens," Stacy said, grinning at Lynn.

"Call them back and tell them I'm okay," her father yelled.

"Too late, Dad. The cops just pulled up in front of the house."

As soon as the paramedics left, Lynn kissed her mother and grandmother goodbye.

"I wish you wouldn't leave already, Lynn. We've hardly had a chance to talk."

"I've really upset Dad. I think it's best if I leave. I'll see you soon. I'm sorry for what happened."

"Please, go talk to your father before you leave," Rosemary pleaded.

Lynn sighed. "Later, Mom. I'll call him later and apologize."

"Lynn, you go talk to him right now."

"Mom, I don't. . ."

"You get your butt in that living room and talk to him. Apologize, you hear. I have to live with him, you know. If you don't tell him you're sorry, he'll be upset all week and he'll drive me crazy." Her mother put her hand on Lynn's back and gave her a little push. "Go."

"All right, I'm going. Jeez, you don't have to shove me."

Lynn went into the living room and stood in front of her father. "Dad?"

"You're blocking the TV. Move."

"I'm sorry, Dad," she said, not moving. "I didn't

mean it."

Her father picked up the remote and hit the mute button. "Of course, you did," he told her. "And, you were right."

Lynn's jaw dropped in surprise. "I was right?" she muttered.

"Yes. We've been doing these blasted lunches for years now. It's time we cut back. Maybe, once a month would be okay. What do you think?"

"I don't. . . I guess. . . I mean. . ."

"Quit stuttering, Lynn."

"I guess it's a good idea."

"Of course, it is. I'll talk to your mother about it. She spends half a day cooking in a hot kitchen, always worrying about you kids getting here on time. It would be good for everyone if we cut back. Your mother could use a day now and then to just relax."

"Well, you know with grandma still here, she wouldn't get a day off to relax," Lynn commented.

"You girls could help her with that, you know. One of you could come over and stay with your grandmother once in a while, so your mother could get out more and do stuff," Joseph said.

"What kind of stuff?" Lynn asked, thoroughly enjoying this conversation with her father.

"How the hell should I know what kind of stuff? The kind of stuff women do when their kids are all grown and out of the house. Play bingo, maybe."

"What about Junior? Couldn't he watch her, too? He lives closer than I do."

Her father hesitated a moment. "I suppose he could. But it would be better if you girls do it."

16

"Why's that?" Lynn asked him.

"I don't know. You're girls. . . You have more in common with her."

"I guess. But, if mom wants to go out, wouldn't you be here to stay with grandma? It's not like she has to have her diapers changed or anything, you know."

Her father stared at her for a second and grinned. "Maybe, not now, but it's only a matter of time."

Lynn laughed. "Well, when the time comes, I think you'll do a great job. Now, getting back to having our Sunday lunches once a month. . . Well, I do think it's a good idea, Dad," Lynn said.

"It will be if you would get your ass here on time. Now, what in the world is your grandmother up to with all that talk about a scooter?"

Lynn looked surprised. Usually, her father didn't show any interest in her grandmother. For him to be inquisitive regarding something Tillie had said was new territory for her.

"She has this crazy idea that she should get a scooter."

"A scooter? Aren't those for kids? She'll kill herself on one of those."

"Not a two-wheel scooter. She wants one of those electric scooters that you sit on and drive. I told her how expensive they are, but she said Medicare will pay for it if she has a note from her doctor."

Her dad pursed his lips, thinking about what Lynn had said. "You know, Lynn, it's not a bad idea."

Lynn looked shocked, as she stared at her father, not believing what he had just said. "You're kidding."

"She falls down a lot, you know."

"I know, dad, but can you see her driving a moving vehicle? She'll kill herself."

"Think about it. They don't go that fast, and it's not like she'll be on the streets. She's not senile, you know."

"You could fool me. She sure acts like it sometimes," Lynn declared.

"It's all a show. She's fine. With a scooter, she could go see her friends that live close by, ride around the block and get some fresh air. . ."

"And, get hit by a car when she crosses the road," Lynn added.

"And, give your mother an occasional break," he continued, ignoring her comment. "I think the whole family should discuss this right now. Go tell your mother and sister to get in here."

Lynn shook her head. "This is not a good idea, Dad."

"One of these days she is going to fall and break a hip. If she's sitting down, she can't fall down," he argued."

"She can fall out of the scooter, you know," Lynn argued.

"Rosemary! Stacy!" her father yelled. "Come in here."

Lynn grinned. "What about Grams? Doesn't she get to add her two cents to this conversation?"

"Tillie! You come in here, too," he shouted. He looked at Lynn and smiled. "There. Happy?" "I take it Junior doesn't get a say about this," Lynn said.

"Do you see him here?"

"Are you going to talk about cutting back on Sunday lunches, too?" Lynn whispered.

"That's the second thing on the agenda," he told her. "Now, sit down and behave yourself."

Three

Lynn threw her purse on the counter and opened the refrigerator door. She grabbed a can of beer, pulled the top off, and took a long swallow.

"God, that tastes good," she said to herself.

Just as she reached inside her purse to take out her phone, it started to vibrate. She glanced at the caller ID and was surprised to see that it was her mother calling her. She was usually napping at this time on Sundays.

"Mom? What's up?"

"Why do you hate me, Lynn?"

"What are you talking about?" Lynn replied. "I don't hate you."

"Well, you must. It isn't bad enough that a day doesn't go by without me worrying about your grandmother staying upright, but now, thanks to you, I have to worry about her driving that bugger machine, too. I thought that at least you would be on my side."

"I was on your side, Mom. I voted against. . ."

"I expect that from your sister, but not you, Lynn. And, I'm sorry that getting together with the family once a week is such a chore. Maybe, we should cancel all the lunches from now on."

"It's not that I don't. . ."

"I don't know what you and your father hatched that up in that living room, but I do know that now I don't get to see my family every Sunday. And, my mother – your grandmother – will probably kill herself on that machine. Thanks a lot."

"Mom, I'm sorry. It's just that dad thought that

it was. . . Mom? Are you still there?"

Lynn looked at her phone, a surprised look on her face. Her mother had hung up on her. She started to call her back but decided it might be better to wait until her mother had cooled off.

She took another swallow of her beer and thought about the conversation the family had after they had finished eating. She better mark her calendar. Now that they were doing Sunday lunches every other week, it would be easy to forget which Sunday was which.

She grabbed a pen out of her purse and looked at the calendar that was on her frig. Not next week but the week after that, if she remembered correctly. She circled the date. It wasn't what she and her dad had hoped for, but it was still a win. Lunch every other week was still better than every week. She was concerned about her mom, though, knowing how badly her feelings had been hurt.

On the other hand, she had voted against her grandmother getting a scooter. "It was a bad idea letting grandma vote," she said to herself, thinking about the fight that had transpired. It was two against two and Grandma had the final vote.

Well, grandma might have won the battle but the war wasn't over. Now, she had to find someone to take her to the doctor to get her note for Medicare. Lynn and her mom weren't going to take her, and she doubted if Stacy would do it. That left her father and there was no way in this world that he would take that old lady anywhere.

I think mom can breathe easy for a while, Lynn

21

decided, as she finished off her beer. There is no way grandma is getting that note.

However - as the saying goes – out of sight, out of mind. And, unfortunately, Junior was out of sight the day the vote took place. He didn't know about the vote and he certainly didn't know that Tillie had an ace up her sleeve. And, that ace had his name on it.

The following Saturday, Rosemary sent out a group text, requesting that her children visit her and their father on Sunday. It was extremely important, was all the text said, giving the three siblings no idea what was up.

"I'm sorry, Stacy, but Buzz has a game on Sunday. I can't make it," Simon told his wife when she mentioned the text to him.

"That's fine," Stacy responded. "She just wants Lynn, Junior, and me there, anyhow. You'll have to take Lisa with you to the game if you don't mind."

"That's fine."

She gave her husband a look.

"What?" he asked her.

"I wish you wouldn't call David Buzz."

"Sorry, I keep forgetting that you don't like it. What time are you going over there?"

Stacy gave him a blank stare. "Huh," she muttered. "I don't know. She didn't say in her text."

"Don't you think you should find out?"

Stacy picked up her phone and sent her mother a text.

Joseph, Jr. looked at the text from his mother and sighed. He had just heard about the vote to cut back on Sunday's dinners from Stacy and he had no intentions of being in the middle of a family fight. He started to text his mom to tell her he had plans he couldn't break. He pulled his finger off the little keyboard and looked out of his living room window, thinking about what to do. "Shit," he said, and typed *i'll be there what time?* and hit send.

"I'm sorry, Nick, but I have to go."

"I've been looking forward to this, Lynn. You finally tell me that we'll be able to spend more time together and now this. What's so important that you have to jump every time your mother wiggles her little finger?"

"Dad and I really hurt her feelings, Nick. I just have to go that's all. She doesn't ask for much, you know. This will be the last time something like this will happen. I promise."

"Well, what am I supposed to do with the other ticket?"

"Ask your sister. Or, how about John? He would enjoy it."

"I guess. You promise, though, that this is the end of breaking dates?"

"I promise. And, from now on I'll have every other Sunday free. Bye."

Lynn ended the call with Nick, hit four on her speed dial, and called her sister.

"Hi," Lynn said when her sister answered her phone.

"I'm on my way out the door. Can I call you back?" Stacy asked.

"Just a fast question. Do you know what time on Sunday?"

"Three."

"Three? That late? Why so late?"

"That's all I know. Gotta go. Love ya," Stacy replied and cut off the call.

Four

"I'm tired. That's all. This house is way too big for just three of us, and it's getting to be way too much work. Your father and I talked this over and we've decided to downsize."

Rosemary looked at the shocked faces of her children and had all she could do to keep a straight face. "Besides, what's the point of keeping this big house if no one is going to come and visit us?" she added.

"I have to admit that I'm stunned at this, Mom. You've never mentioned anything about moving before now. Exactly how does grandma feel about you selling her house?" Junior asked.

"I'm right here, Junior," Tillie said. "I can still talk, you know."

"Sorry, Grandma. It's just that I'm surprised that you want to move. After all, you've spent most of your life in this house."

"She's fine with it," Rosemary said.

"Well, I'm not," Stacy declared. "How about you, Lynn? Are you okay with it?"

"Of course, I'm not okay with it."

"I'm not either," Tillie declared.

Rosemary glanced over at her mother and frowned. "You said you were going to keep quiet, Mother."

"Well, maybe I changed my mind. Look at how upset the kids are."

"Dad, are you okay with this?" Stacy asked.

Her father shrugged his shoulders and looked

away.

Lynn studied her mother's face, wondering what was actually behind all of this. She glanced over at her father and realized he was totally uncomfortable with this conversation. "This is about the Sunday lunches, isn't it?" she said, quietly."

Her mother gave her a dirty look. "No, it's not, Lynn. That's behind us. It was all settled last week if you recall. I don't know why you're bringing that up again. We just want to move, that's all."

"Well, I've changed my mind," Tillie blurted out. "If we move, I won't have any place to put my scooter."

Rosemary rolled her eyes, exasperated with her mother. "You don't have to worry about that, Mother, because you are not getting a scooter."

"Of course, I am, Rosemary. We voted on it last Sunday, remember? And, I talked to my doctor, and they are taking care of the paperwork for me. I don't have to do one thing. It will probably take a while to hear back from them, but Junior said it was looking good. Didn't you, Junior?"

Rosemary looked at her son, trying to hold back her temper. "You did this?"

Junior turned red in the face. "Did what? All I did was talk to grandma. She asked me to find out what she needed to do to get a scooter, so I checked it out on the internet and told her. I'm confused, Grandma. Is there something going on that I don't know about?"

"Nothing is going on, Sweetie. Don't you worry about your mother? She must have forgotten that we voted on this."

"When did you talk to her," Rosemary asked her son.

"She called me Monday morning. Dad was at work and you were out shopping. I think grandma said you were grocery shopping. Hey, I didn't do anything wrong."

"Does anyone want some coffee?" Lynn asked."

"No!" everyone yelled in unison.

"Jeez. Sorry," Lynn said.

"All right, that's it. I've had enough of this. I want everyone to be quiet and listen," Joseph said loudly, as he got up out of his chair. He waited for a second, making sure he had everyone's attention. "This has gotten totally out of hand. Your mother has hardly slept all week. You hurt – no, we all hurt her feelings last Sunday. The truth is that nobody wants to move. It seemed like a good idea, but we were wrong. I'm sorry, Rosemary, but we are not moving and that's final."

"But, you agreed," Rosemary said. "You said that we. . ."

"I know what I said, but I was wrong. I don't want to move and Tillie wants to stay here in her own home. And, I'm pretty sure that you do, too. So, let's continue our Sunday get-togethers, just like always. Only, let's have them three Sundays a month instead of every other week. What do you say, Rosemary? Can you live with that?"

Rosemary thought for a second and, then, smiled.

"I guess that sounds okay," she told him.

"Now, your mother will make a schedule of

which Sundays you should be here and give each of you a copy. That way, you will know how to plan in advance."

"But I don't know if I. . ."

"Quiet, Junior. I'm not finished. Also, Rosemary, I want you to hire a woman to come in once a week and clean this house. This is a big house and it's becoming too much work for you to handle by yourself."

"I'm not sure if I'm comfortable with that, Joseph," Rosemary said.

"Then get comfortable. And, finally - and, I mean finally - I don't want to hear any more about that damn scooter, you hear? If Medicare approves Tillie's application for a mobility scooter, I see no reason why she can't have one. We voted on it as a family and that was settled a week ago. If there's a problem with it, down the road, we'll get rid of the damn thing."

"Well, I guess that would be okay," Rosemary said, giving Joseph a big smile.

"Agreed, everyone?" he asked.

"No," Tillie exclaimed. "I don't agree. You're not going to get rid of my scooter."

"Good. Then, it's settled," he said, ignoring Tillie. "Now, Lynn, how about you go and make that pot of coffee?"

As Lynn stood up to go to the kitchen, she glanced over at her mother. She looks like a flippin' cat that just swallowed the canary. That sly fox planned this whole thing, she thought. She looked at her father and wondered if he was in on it. She smiled sweetly at her father and said, "Dad, can I talk to you in the kitchen?"

He shook his head no.

"Dad?"

"Not now, Lynn. Maybe a little later. Now be a good girl and go make that coffee, will you? By the way, your mother has made dessert for everyone."

"I don't know why we even bothered with that voting crap. There's no democracy in this house, that's for sure," Lynn muttered, as she walked out of the room.

"Is there something you wanted to say, Lynn?" her father called to her.

"You want your coffee black or with cream?"

"The cake was delicious, Mom."

"Thank you, Junior."

"Pineapple upside-down cake, right?"

"Yes, that's right."

"What gave it away?" Stacy asked him, grinning. "The pineapple or the fact that it was upside down?"

"It wasn't upside down," Junior snapped. "The pineapple was on top."

"That's enough, you two," Rosemary said, reprimanding her children.

"Well, I've got to get going," Stacy said, as she pushed her chair away from the table. "Oh, I need to know when you plan on having lunch again. Is it next Sunday or a week from next Sunday?"

"Next Sunday," her mother said, without hesitation. "I'm making brisket."

"Oh, Mom, not next Sunday? I'm not sure I can make it. I've already made plans with Nick," Lynn whined.

"Bring him along," her father told her.

"Well, that's a first," Stacy said, surprised that her father would suggest that Lynn bring one of her boyfriends to dinner.

"I've got to go, too," Junior said. "But there's something you should know, Mom." He glanced over at the living room, making sure that Tillie was asleep on the couch and couldn't hear him.

"What's that?"

"The chances of grandma getting a scooter are slim to none. She's still able to walk on her own and she doesn't live alone. I don't think she fits the criteria for Medicare to pay for it. So, stop worrying about it. Okay?"

Rosemary gave him a big smile. "Oh, thank you, Junior. I wish I had known this before." She gave a little laugh. "To think I've done all that worrying for nothing. Thank you, thank you."

"See, I told you to stop worrying about it," Joseph told his wife.

"Well, that's good news, I guess," Stacy said, as she headed out the door. "Bye, all. See you next week."

"You're very quiet, Lynn," Rosemary said.

"I was trying to decide if I should ask Nick to come next week."

"And....?" Junior said, grinning.

"I don't know if he could take it, that's all. I can barely handle being here. How can I subject him to all of this?" she answered, sweeping her arm from left to right.

Junior laughed. "Bring him along, Lynn. Let's

see what he's made of. Of course, there's always the chance that we might break him, but that's the risk you have to take."

"What are you children talking about?" Rosemary asked, looking confused.

"Nothing, Mom," Lynn replied. "I've got to go."

"Me, too," Junior said, getting up from the table. "I'll walk you out," he told his sister.

Lynn and Junior kissed their mother and father goodbye and headed towards the door.

"You know, Junior, there is always that slim chance that Medicare will approve grandma's request and she'll get that scooter after all," Lynn said, grinning.

Rosemary's head jerked up and she looked at her husband. "What did she just say, Joseph? There's a chance she'll get it? Is that what she said?"

Joseph watched Lynn and Junior leave the house and waited until the door was shut. Then, he closed his eyes and put his face in his hands. He let out a big sigh and fought the desire to break down and cry.

RED . . . . Susan L Pare'

August, 2017

Five

Sergeant Matt Haase hung up the phone and sighed. He ran his fingers through his hair and decided it was time for another haircut. It seemed he was getting his hair cut a lot more than he used to. And, when he thought about it, he realized that he now needed to trim his nose hair at least once a week.

He glanced over at Sergeant Lee Wong. "How often do you have to trim your ear hair?"

Wong looked up. "Are you talking to me?"

"How often do you trim your ear hair?" he asked Wong again.

Wong grinned. "What brought that on?"

"I just got another call from Mrs. Larson. I guess I was thinking about growing old and how much more maintenance our bodies require than they used to."

"Speak for yourself, man. My body is in the best shape ever. You're the one getting old and fat – not me."

"I'm not fat! And, I'm not old. I'm only forty-two."

"Really? You look a lot older than that," Wong commented, grinning.

"Thanks a lot," Haase said. "Do you want to take a ride?"

"Where to?" Wong inquired.

"The Larson's house."

"Is Tillie missing again?" Wong asked.

"Yup. She took off on that damn scooter to visit a friend. She was supposed to be back an hour ago."

"And, did Mrs. Larson check with the friend to see if she was still there?" Wong asked.

"She did. Tillie left her house way over an hour ago. Mrs. Larson drove up and down the streets. She can't find her."

"Yeah, I'll come along. It's a nice day for a ride."

Rosemary Larson was standing on the front porch when Haase and Wong pulled up to her house. She waved, as the officers stepped out of the squad car.

"Good afternoon, Mrs. Larson," Haase said. "Have you heard anything about where your mother might be hiding this time?"

"Absolutely nothing at all. I've driven up and down the streets and phoned everyone I can think of. No one has seen or heard from her since she left Minnie William's house. I'm at my wits end with that woman," Rosemary said, trying to hold back her emotions.

"It will be all right. We always find her," Haase told her. "Shall we go inside?"

"I'm sorry. Where are my manners? Come in."

"Please, have a seat," Rosemary said, as they entered the living room. "Can I get you anything? Coffee? Tea?"

"I could go for a glass of water if it's not too much bother," Sergeant Wong said.

"Of course. I'll be right back," Rosemary replied, as she scurried out of the room.

"Nice house," Wong commented.

"It is." Haase agreed.

"Have they lived here long?" Wong asked.

"It's Tillie's house. She's lived here for over sixty

years. She was friends with my grandmother, way back in the olden days."

"Really?" Wong said, surprised. "That's a long time."

"Sure is. Her husband died a few years back and Rosemary and her husband moved in. You know, to take care of her."

Wong grinned. "I don't think that woman needs a whole lot of taking care of. She seems to manage on her own quite well."

"I heard she also manages to fall down a lot. Mrs. Larson worries about her," Haase said.

"Did Tillie have any other kids?" Wong inquired.

"She had a son, but he passed away a long time ago." He thought for a moment. "It must be at least ten or twelve years now."

"Cancer?" Wong asked.

"He got killed in a motorcycle accident. I think that's one of the reasons Rosemary hates to see her mother riding on that three-wheeled scooter. It reminds her of what happened to her brother." He glanced towards the kitchen. "How long does it take to get a glass of water?"

Wong shrugged. "Beats me."

"Is everything okay in there, Mrs. Larson?" Haase yelled.

Rosemary walked into the living room and handed Sergeant Wong a glass of water. "I'm sorry it took so long. I just had a phone call from the manager of the Dairy Queen. He said mother is there. I have to go get her."

"We'll drive you over there and make sure she

gets home okay."

"Would you? I'd really appreciate that."

"How old is your mother, Mrs. Larson?" Wong asked her.

"Please, call me Rosemary," she said smiling. "My mother is eighty."

"How is her health? Does she have any problems we should know about?"

"Physically she is in excellent condition for her age. Her balance is off a little. That's probably why she tends to fall down. She has a little arthritis, of course. But, what person that age doesn't? My goodness, even I have a touch of arthritis. And, as you probably already know, she has a bad case of selective hearing."

"What is selective hearing?" Wong asked, confused by her comment.

"She only hears what she wants to hear," Rosemary told him.

Sergeant Wong smiled. "Ah, yes. My grandmother had that, too. It seems to come with age."

"I'm not sure about that. My husband seems to have contracted a case of it, also."

"And, how old is he?" Wong inquired.

Rosemary gave him a baffled look, then, smiled. "I see your point, Sergeant. I guess he is getting up there. He'll be retiring in a few years."

"Let's go get your mother, shall we?" Sergeant Haase asked.

Ten minutes later Rosemary, accompanied by the two policemen, walked into the Dairy Queen on Park Avenue and looked around. They had noticed

Tillie's scooter parked outside the entrance but did not see her in the building.

Rosemary watched Sergeant Wong walk over to the counter and say something to the young girl behind the counter. The employee shook her head no. Wong said something else and the employee shrugged her shoulders and turned away.

"She doesn't know where she went," Wong said, as he approached Rosemary and Haase.

"What do you mean she doesn't know where she went?" Rosemary exclaimed. "The manager said she would be right here." She looked up at Sergeant Haase. "What should we do?"

"Don't get excited, Mrs. Larson. We'll find her. Let me look around outside."

"She can't be too far," Rosemary said, as Haase walked away. "She wouldn't leave her scooter behind."

"Don't worry," Wong commented. "How hard can it be to find an old lady?"

"You don't know my mother."

"Don't you think she's kinda old to be riding all over town on that thing?" Wong said, indicating the scooter. "I thought they were more for getting around in the house."

"They are," Rosemary said. "But, it's perfectly legal to ride them on the sidewalks."

"Maybe it's time to get rid of it."

"Oh, you think it's time, do you?" Rosemary uttered. "Well, don't you think I haven't tried? It's like a bad penny. You can try to get rid of it, but it always comes back."

"What do you mean, it always comes back?"

Wong asked. "

"We actually donated it to a medical supply service. They picked it up from the house and drove away with it. I watched them. I saw them load it onto their truck and drive away," Rosemary said, her voice getting loud. "And – God only knows how - the next day it was on our front porch. I don't know how it got there. Nobody knows. Oh, that's not true. My mother knows. She just won't tell us, but she knows."

"She must know somebody. . ."

"No, she doesn't. I checked. One time we hid it in our neighbor's garage. We figured we'd wait until morning and then tell her it had been stolen. When we got up that morning, she was riding around in the house on it. No, Sergeant, it just keeps coming back. We gave up on trying to get rid of it. Of course, we have discussed having a big bonfire to see if it will burn." She let out a big sigh. "It's just easier to let her keep the damn thing than to argue with her. Sorry, I didn't mean to swear."

"I've heard worse. But someone must be helping her," Wong declared.

"You'd think, wouldn't you? But, there's no one that we could find that helped. . ." She looked up as Sergeant Haase came around the corner of the building.

"Well?" Wong asked.

Haase shook his head no. "I've looked all over. I even checked in the washrooms. Right now, I have no idea where she could have gone."

"Oh, my god," Rosemary cried out. "We've got to find her."

"We will. Right now, let's get you home. Wong, let's take that scooter with us. It folds up, doesn't it?" he asked Rosemary.

"Where could she be?" Rosemary muttered, ignoring his question.

Sergeant Haase took her arm. "Sergeant Wong, I'm pretty sure it folds up and will fit in our trunk. Put it in the car, will you?"

"We can't leave here," Rosemary said softly. "I can't leave without my mother." She pulled her arm away.

"We need to go, Mrs. Larson. Your mother might even be back at your house by now."

"Let me try calling her again before we leave. Maybe, she'll answer this time."

The sergeant waited while Rosemary called her mother's phone. She looked at him and shook her head. "She's still not answering."

"The scooter is ringing." Wong walked over to the scooter and reached into a small storage compartment. He hesitated a moment, then pulled out a cell phone and held it in the air for Haase to see.

Rosemary's knees went weak, and she grabbed for Haase's arm. "I need to sit down," she murmured.

The Sergeants dropped Rosemary and the scooter off at her house, promising to put out an all-points bulletin and to call her as soon as they knew something. She glanced at the grandfather's clock, as she entered the house, noting that her mother had been missing for almost three hours.

Rosemary went into the kitchen and put the

kettle on, so she could make herself a cup of tea. She tried to decide if she should call Joseph and the kids to let them know what was going on. She decided to give it another half hour or so, while she tried to figure out where her mother could be this time.

"That damn scooter," she muttered to herself. She jumped as her phone rang, scaring her. The caller ID said unknown, however, Rosemary recognized that it was a Columbus phone number.

"Hello?" she answered.

"Where the hell is my scooter? The girl in the Dairy Queen said you came and got it. You and some cops. What the hell, Rosemary? How am I supposed to get home?"

"Mother, are you okay? I've been so worried about you. Where are you?"

"Why do you insist on doing these things? Just once, I'd like to take a little ride and not have you chasing around town looking for me. Now, you have to come and get me. This has got to end, Rosemary. I mean it."

"I was worried about you. You left Minnie's house almost three hours ago. What was I supposed to do? For all I knew, you could have been lying in a ditch someplace."

"Quit the melodramatics. Just come and get me."

Rosemary's jaw dropped. Her mother had just hung up the phone without telling her where she was. Rosemary jumped as the tea kettle started to whistle, startling her. She sat down, put her head on the kitchen table, and started to cry.

She started to reach for her phone as it rang again but, then, she hesitated. She knew she had to answer it, but every fiber of her being yelled at her to ignore it – to toss it down the garbage disposal and grind it to little pieces.

"Hello?" she said softly, as her curiosity won out and she answered the phone.

"Sergeant Wong here, Mrs. Larson. We just got a call from the bartender at Kurth's Brewery. It seems that your mother has been there for some time now. She's fine, but it seems that a phone call she just made has upset her. He thought it best to call us and let us know."

"She's in a tavern?" Rosemary said, shocked. "She's been in at Kurth's all this time?"

"Well, we don't know if it's been the whole time. It seems she went to the Dairy Queen to get some ice cream and ran into an old friend. They decided to have a beer and she lost track of time."

"She's drinking? I'm sitting home worried sick about her and she's out having a good time?"

"Are you okay?" Wong asked.

"No. I'm upset. I mean, I'm really upset. I don't think I should drive right now. Thank you for letting me know where she is. I'll call my husband and tell him to go get her when he gets off of work. Until then, she can just sit and wait."

"I'll be glad to pick her up for you, Mrs. Larson."

"You would do that? That's very nice of you."

"I'd be happy to. Why don't you fix yourself a nice cup of tea and settle down? I should have your mother home within the half-hour."

"That sounds nice, Sergeant. I think I'll do just that. And, thank you."

"We aim to please. I'll see you a bit."

Rosemary ended her phone call and walked out of her house onto the back porch. She lived on N. Lewis St. and her yard butted up to the banks of the Crawfish River. She noticed that the river was unusually high today, most likely due to the heavy rains of the past few nights.

It wouldn't take much for someone to drive their little ass scooter right into that river and drown, she thought. I wonder how long it would take to find the body.

"Thank you so much for bringing her home, Sergeant Wong."

"My pleasure. I'm just glad that we found her safe and sound. Is there anything else you need?" he asked her.

"I need to get rid of that scooter. That's what I need."

"Did you ever consider removing the ramp so she couldn't get down from the porch onto the sidewalk? Wong asked.

"Oh, we did that after the second time she disappeared. That time she was missing for half a day."

"Then, why did you put it back?"

Rosemary looked pained. "She tried to ride it down the steps but it tipped over, and she spent three days in the hospital. We thought about getting rid of the damn thing while she was recovering, but all she worried about was if her scooter was okay. We didn't have the heart to do it and Joseph put the ramp back up."

"You do have your hands full with her, don't you? But I have to say that I think she's still a pretty sharp lady. We had a good conversation on the way over here. She seems to know everything that is going on."

Rosemary smirked. 'Oh, I see she's suckered you in, too. Well, Sergeant, you don't have to live with her day after day and take care of her and worry about her like. . ." Rosemary took a deep breath and started to sob.

"I'm so sorry," Wong said, looking around the room as if help would suddenly appear. "Please. I didn't mean to upset you."

"What's she crying for?"

Wong turned to see Tillie standing in the doorway, a concerned look on her face.

"She's upset because she was worried that something had happened to you," he told her.

"Oh, that. Well, I'm sure she'll get over it. I'm gonna take a nap before dinner. Beer always makes me tired. Thanks again for the ride," she said, smiling, as she turned and walked out of the kitchen.

"Well, I guess I'll be going, then," Wong told Rosemary, who was still sobbing.

As Wong started to leave the house, Joseph Larson came through the front door. He saw the scooter sitting in the hallway, looked at Wong, glanced over at Tillie who was lying on the couch, and heard his wife crying in the kitchen. "Tillie?" he asked Wong,

as he passed him in the entry.
"Yup," Wong replied

Six

"This sandwich is very good, Rosemary," Tillie remarked. "Of course, I don't see how a sandwich could be bad. They're so easy to make. I enjoy a good sandwich every so often. Unless it's a tongue sandwich. I hate tongue."

Rosemary, who was sitting across the table from her mother, didn't respond.

"Or, if the bread is dried out," Tillie continued. "Nothing worse than dried-out old bread. How about you, Joseph? Are you enjoying these sandwiches that Rosemary made for our supper?"

Joseph glanced over at his wife, who remained emotionless. "I guess."

"That's a good thing, seeing as how you have them for lunch every day," Tillie said, taking a bite of her ham and cheese sandwich. "I would think you'd get tired of them," she said, as she swallowed.

"Well, I haven't yet. Rosemary mixes it up so they are different every day. I like that," he told Tillie, keeping an eye on his wife.

"Maybe, we should have them for lunch on Sundays, too. I'm sure everyone would enjoy them. Maybe we could have a peanut butter day. You know, like peanut butter and jelly or peanut butter and bologna. Then, there are also peanut butter and banana sandwiches. Or peanut butter and dill pickles. That's always a favorite."

"I doubt that Rosemary is going to make sandwiches for Sunday lunch. However, I do think we arc fortunate that she took the time to make anything

47

for dinner. I imagine she's quite tired after the day she had." Joseph told her.

"Fiddlesticks. If she's tired, it's because she ran all over the neighborhood looking for me. That was her choice. Don't put the blame on me. Besides, she could have ordered a pizza. A pizza would have been a lot better than these sandwiches."

Rosemary took a sip of her iced tea and set the glass down. Joseph could tell that her boiling point had just about been reached, and he knew she was about to lose it. "It's a long ride from our house to the Dairy Queen, isn't it?" he asked Tillie. "How long did it take you to get there?"

Tillie grinned. "Well, I tried to keep it below the 15-mph mark. That stands for fifteen miles per hour."

"I know that," Joseph remarked.

"I have to admit, though, that Red can move out pretty good and I had to slow down a few times."

Joseph looked confused. "Red?" What is red?"

"My scooter. I named him Red. I thought you knew that."

Rosemary rolled her eyes and sighed. "Give me strength," she muttered under her breath.

"I don't know how far it is, Joseph," Tillie said, as she shot her daughter a dirty look. "But I made it in under thirty minutes."

"Impressive," he commented. "But, you know, Tillie, you shouldn't be riding on the streets."

"Oh," she exclaimed. "I don't. I stay on the sidewalks. I mean, I cross the streets, of course, but that's the only time I ride Red on them. I'm very careful, you know."

"I'm glad to hear that," Joseph told her. "We sure don't want anything to happen to you."

Rosemary glanced over at her husband and shook her head in disgust.

"I understand you visited Minnie today. How's she doing?" he asked, changing the subject.

"She's got a few problems. I'm in better shape than she is. Did you know she's just a year older than me?"

"Really? I didn't know that," Joseph said, looking at his wife, realizing that he wasn't making things any better.

"Yup. It won't be long now," Tillie commented.

Joseph thought for a second. "What won't be long?"

"Before she kicks the bucket. You know – bites the dust, cashes in her chips, meets the grim reaper, is worm food . . ."

"I get it," Joseph said, smiling. "So, how did you go? You know, to the Dairy Queen."

"It's a simple ride, Joseph. I took Lewis to Fuller, made a left on Fuller to Park, crossed the street there, and it was a straight shot to the Dairy Queen. But you already know that, don't you?"

"It's also a straight shot to Kurth's Brewery, isn't it, Mother?" Rosemary shouted, obviously having reached her boiling point.

Tillie, surprised by her daughter's outburst, dropped her sandwich onto the floor. She looked down at it and sat back in her chair. "You don't have to yell, Rosemary," she said quietly. "If you have something to say, then, say it. But, use your church voice, will you?"

"I'm sorry I yelled, but you scared me today, Mother. You can't just take off and not let me know where you are."

"I forget sometimes, Rosemary, that you think I'm your child. I forget that you expect me to check in every hour that I'm not in your sight."

"I worry about you."

"Well, stop. When the day comes that I don't know my name or where I live. . ." Tilly took a deep breath. "Then, you can treat me like a child. But, until then, please let me live the few years I have left in peace."

"Fine!" Rosemary yelled.

"Good. Then, that's settled." Tillie looked across the table at Joseph. "I saw an old friend today, Joseph. Do you remember John Hobson?"

"I've heard of him. I never knew him personally. He used to be the president of Farmers and Merchants Bank, here in town, I believe. Of course, that was a long time ago."

"Right. I went to school with one of his sons, Lowell. Anyway, Lowell was at the Dairy Queen and we got to talking. The poor soul lost his wife twenty years ago. He never remarried."

"Really?" Joseph said. "Well, not everyone takes that big step the second time."

"Anyway, he asked if I wanted to go next door and get a beer at Kurth's and I said yes. I can't remember the last time I was there. I didn't even know they were still open."

"I think they are only open on Wednesday and

Friday."

"I know that now. Anyway, we started talking and we just lost track of time. When I finally realized how late it was, I was going to come home and. . ." She took a swallow of her tea. "Well, Red was gone and I was stuck there. I figured your wife had something to do with it and guess what? She did. She hates it when I enjoy myself."

Rosemary laid her napkin on her plate and excused herself. She walked out onto the back porch, tears running down her face.

"You know, Tillie, she worries about you," Joseph said. "Ever since you got that scooter. . ."

"Red," Tillie interrupted.

"Right. Well, ever since you got Red, she worries that something will happen to you. If you kept your phone with you and checked in when you change your plans, she'd be fine. Do you think you could do that, Tillie?"

Tillie looked away. This was one of the longest conversations she could remember having with him in years. "You're not going to try to get rid of Red again, are you?"

Joseph looked surprised. "Of course not. I would never do that."

Tillie eyed him, staring at his expression. He thinks I'm as senile as Rosemary does, she thought to herself. "If you promise that you won't ever do anything to get rid of Red, I'll promise to keep my phone with me and check in with Rosemary if I change my plans."

"That sounds like a deal. One other thing, Tillie,"

he whispered. "Do you think you could apologize to her? You know, just say you're sorry about today. It would make her feel better."

Tillie smiled and leaned forward in her chair. "How about this?" she whispered back. "No."

Joseph sat back in his chair, surprised at her answer. "Why not? It would make everything all right again."

Tillie looked through the screen door and saw Rosemary standing on the porch, looking out towards the river. "You should go talk to Rosemary. See if she'll apologize to me. Then, everything will be all right again."

Joseph pushed his chair back and stood up. "I give up. I don't even know why I try with you two," he muttered, as he walked away from the table.

"By the way, would you tell Rosemary that I won't be here on Sunday? I have a date," Tillie said, grinning.

Seven

"Where's Grandma?" Lynn asked her dad.

"Your grandmother is on a date," he replied. "And, don't mention her in front of your mother."

Lynn looked shocked and amused at the same time. "You're kidding?" she said, trying to hold back a laugh. "With who? Is it someone I know?"

"Who's on a date?" Stacy asked as she walked into the living room.

"Grandma," Lynn told her.

Stacy grinned. "No kidding? Good for her. Who's she on a date with?"

Both women looked at their father, grinning.

"Spill the beans, Dad," Stacy said. "Tell us everything."

"Shh. Your mother will hear you."

"So what? Doesn't she know about it?"

"Oh, she knows about it, all right. I'm telling you, girls, it's been hell here the past few days. Your mother isn't talking to your grandmother and I'm right in the middle of it. 'Tell your wife this' and 'tell my mother that'. I've become a damn messenger. The worst thing that ever happened to this family is Red."

"Red? Red who?" Lynn asked, looking confused.

"Red. Her scooter," Joseph said. "That's its name. Red."

Stacy grinned. "So, it has a name now, does it? That's cute."

"No, it's not cute. She took off on the damn thing on Friday and didn't come back for hours. Your mother was worried sick and she called the cops and they found the scooter, but not your grandmother."

"But they eventually did find her, didn't they?" Lynn asked her dad.

"Yes. No. I mean they didn't really find her. When your grandmother came out of Kurth's, her scooter was missing, so she called your mother. She got mad and hung up without telling your mother where she was. So, actually, it was the bartender who called the cops to let them know she was there. Then, the cops brought her home."

"What in the world was she doing in Kurth's?" Stacy said.

Joseph sat back in his chair and sighed. "I guess this is all a little confusing, isn't it?"

"A little," Lynn replied.

"You think?" Stacy asked.

"She met an old friend at the Dairy Queen and they went next door to Kurth's to have a beer. She lost track of time and she was gone so long she scared the crap out of your mother."

"Who drove her to the Dairy Queen?" Lynn asked.

"No one. She rode Red there." He looked up, as the door opened and Junior walked into the house. "It's a miracle. Everyone is on time today."

Junior glanced into the living room. "Hi. What's going on?"

"Whatever you do, don't mention grandma today," Lynn told him.

"Did something happen to grandma?" he asked, looking concerned.

"She's fine. But there's a situation going on,"

Lynn told him.

"Stacy, go see if your mother needs some help in the kitchen," her father said.

"I don't want to. I might miss something," she whined.

"Go help your mother," he insisted.

"Oh, all right," Stacy said, pouting as she stood and walked towards the kitchen.

A few moments later, she was back in the living room, grinning.

"What's so funny," Lynn asked.

"Lunch is ready. Mom said everyone should sit down at the table."

"I don't smell any food cooking," Junior said, as he stood up to go to the table.

"Me either," Lynn said.

"Just go sit down and, whatever you do, don't talk about your grandmother," Joseph said.

"The table isn't set," Junior said, as he pulled out a chair and sat down at the dining room table.

Rosemary walked out of the kitchen and placed some paper napkins and paper plates in the middle of the table. She turned and walked back into the kitchen. A few seconds later she returned, carrying a tray with a pitcher of lemonade and paper cups. She smiled, as she set the tray down on the table. "Hello, girls. I'm so glad you could make it. How are you, Junior?"

Her three children murmured hello, totally confused by their mother's actions.

"Lynn, would you like to pour everyone a glass of

lemonade?" Rosemary walked back into the kitchen, picked up a large serving platter, and returned to the table. "Help yourselves. There's a variety to choose from," she said, as she placed the tray down in the middle of the table. "I'll see you later. I'm going for a walk."

Rosemary turned her back on her family, smiling as she walked to the front door, opened it, and walked out of the house.

No one said a word, as they all stared at a serving tray piled full of sandwiches.

Lynn and Stacy had cleared the table, which involved nothing more than throwing out a lot of paper and washing the tray that had held the sandwiches.

Joseph had just finished explaining to his kids why their mother was so unhappy. "I don't know what to do. I've never seen your mother this upset. All I've had to eat since Friday are sandwiches. I was hoping that, with you kids coming today, she'd cook a meal," he told them. "Your grandmother tries talking to her, but she won't answer her. She's acting like her mother isn't even there."

"Have you met this man, Lowell Dobson?" Junior asked his father.

"What has that got to do with anything?" his father replied. "The fight started long before Dobson was mentioned."

"Yes, I know. But, is grandma safe with him?" Junior inquired.

"He seems like a nice enough chap. He's around your grandmother's age and they've known each other since school."

"Did grandma mention where they were going today?" Junior asked. "I could go check and see if they're okay."

"No. Don't even think of it. Tillie said that they were going to get a fast burger somewhere and, then, they were going to the Senior Center to play bingo. I don't think there's anything to worry about."

"He drives?" Lynn asked.

"I guess you could say that," Joseph said, looking away.

Junior gave him a strange look. "Well, does he or doesn't he, Dad? Did he pick grandma up or what?"

"In a sense, he did."

"What are you talking about?" Lynn said, wondering what was wrong with her father.

"Forget about your grandmother and tell me what I should do. I can't live on sandwiches for the rest of my life."

"I think we should go look for mom," Lynn said.

"Your mother is fine," Joseph said. "She's been puttering around in the back yard for the past forty-five minutes."

"Junior, go get her. We need to talk to her about this. Ask her to come in," Stacy told him.

"She won't talk about it. I've tried," their father said.

"Junior?"

"You go. I'm not getting involved in this," he said.

"Come on, Lynn, let's go get mom," Stacy said.

Junior waited until the two women had left the

room. He looked over at his dad. "So, tell me."

"What?"

"About that Lowell guy. Does he drive or not?"

"Oh, he drives, all right." Joseph hesitated a moment. "Did you know that your grandmother calls her scooter Red?" he finally said.

"I heard that. Why?"

"Well, Mr. Dobson calls his scooter Blue."

Junior gave his father a questioning look, and, then, grinned as he realized what his father was saying. "No," he said, laughing.

"Yes," his father replied. "Oh, yes."

"Wouldn't it be funny if they had a friend with a white one?" Junior commented, grinning. "How patriotic would that be?"

It took a while, but Rosemary finally broke down and agreed to talk to her mother when she got home from her date. She admitted that she knew the entire argument with her mother was childish and that, perhaps – just perhaps – she had overreacted.

"How about a pizza?" Junior asked, now that everyone seemed more relaxed and ready to move on to new topics. "I don't know about the rest of you, but I'm starving."

No one said anything.

"My treat," he added.

"Sounds good. I could go for a slice," Stacy said.

"Me, too," Lynn added.

"I guess I could go make something to eat, " Rosemary said, feeling guilty about serving only sandwiches for lunch.

"No, Mom," Junior said. "You're done in the kitchen for today." He looked at his father. "Dad?"

Joseph looked up at his son. "What?"

"Could you go for some pizza?"

"I guess. What kind?"

"Any kind you'd like."

"Meat lovers is good. Get that," Joseph said.

"I don't eat meat," Stacy said. "Get a vegetarian pizza, too."

"When did you stop eating meat?" Lynn asked, surprised.

"For crying out loud, Lynn. I quit ages ago. You know that," Stacy said.

"Really? You ate a ham and cheese sandwich a couple of hours ago."

"I did not," Stacy said, adamantly.

"I saw you. Junior, you saw her eat a ham and cheese sandwich, didn't you?" Lynn asked

"How should I know what she ate? Who do you think I am? The sandwich police?" he replied, grinning.

"That's enough, girls," Joseph said loudly. "We don't need to have another battle over something as stupid as who ate what. One dumb fight a week is enough, don't you think?"

"What's that supposed to mean?" Rosemary asked, obviously getting upset over her husband's remark.

"Nothing. It meant absolutely nothing," Joseph replied. "I'm sorry I said that. Just forget it, will you?"

"I think I'll go home," Stacy said. "Simon is most likely home with the kids by now. I imagine they're hungry and will want something to eat."

"You aren't going to stay for pizza?" Junior asked her.

"No, I've got to get going."

"It is getting late. I guess I'll go, too," Lynn said.

"It's only three-thirty, Stacy. Oh, I get it. You've got a hot date with Nick. How's that going, by the way?" Junior inquired.

"There is no Nick. We broke up."

"You do seem to have trouble keeping a man," her brother said. "Maybe, you should take some lessons from Stacy. She seems to know how to hold on to a man."

"Screw you, Junior," Lynn blurted out.

"Junior, apologize to your sister," Rosemary ordered.

"She knows I'm just joking," he said.

"Junior. Apologize."

"I'm sorry, Lynn. I didn't mean to hurt your feelings."

"I'm off," Stacy said, as she grabbed her purse and headed for the door. "See ya. Thanks for lunch, Mom."

Lynn grinned. "I'm leaving, too. Thanks for an interesting Sunday, Mom. It's definitely been one for the books. Say hi to grandma for me. Bye, Dad. Junior."

Joseph shot his daughter a dirty look. "You just had to get in one last dig, didn't you?"

Lynn looked shocked. "What did I say?" she said as she walked out of the house, not waiting for an answer.

Junior, looking confused, looked at his father. "Do you still want pizza?"

"Go home, Junior," his father said, picked up the remote, and turned on the TV.

"I'm going to church to pray," Rosemary told Joseph, trying to be heard over the noise of the TV.

Joseph hit the mute button. "What in the world for?"

"I need to pray for this family. I need to pray for strength to be more patient with my mother."

"You are patient, Rosemary. You're a wonderful daughter."

"And, I need to pray for snow."

Confused by her last remark, Joseph thought for a moment before saying anything. "Did you say snow?" he finally asked. "You want to pray for snow? Did I hear that right?"

"You did."

"You know, it's August, don't you?"

"Miracles happen. Maybe winter will come early this year and then. . ." She looked away.

"And, then, your mother can't ride Red outside," Joseph interrupted. "Is that what you were going to say?"

"Yes. She'll have to stay in the house and I won't be spending all my time worrying about her. At least, I'd have some peace for a few months."

"Well, maybe I'll put some snow chains on Red's tires. How do you like those apples?"

Rosemary spun around to see her mother standing in the doorway. "Mother," she uttered, her face turning red. "When did you get home?"

61

October, 2017

RED . . . . Susan L Pare'

Eight

Tillie was seated on a huge overstuffed couch, watching the last of the logs burn out in Lowell's fireplace. She reached over, picked up her cup, and took a sip of hot tea.

Lowell, who was sitting across from her in a matching chair, closed a photo album and sighed. "Sorry, Tillie. I didn't mean to get so serious, but looking at these pictures always brings me down."

"Understandable. And, there's nothing to apologize for. I lost my husband and a son. I don't think it's something that you ever get over. I still say good-night to John and Jacob after I say my prayers and turn out the lights."

"I do that, too. But at least you still have family that loves you."

"Most of the time, I do. But I figure there are days they wish I would just go away for good. Anyway, did you find that picture you were looking for?"

"No. It must be in a different album. I'll see if I can find it later. Are you hungry?"

Tillie smiled. "We only ate an hour ago, Lowell."

Lowell glanced at his watch. "You're right. I don't know why I'm so hungry."

"I've never known anyone who can eat ten times a day and not gain weight. I'd be as big as a house if I did that."

Lowell smiled. "I'd love you no matter how big you were."

Tillie was silent, watching the last embers of the fire slowly fade away. "Fire's almost out," she sighed. "I hate this time of year when it gets dark so early."

"I'll go with you when you leave and make sure you get home okay," Lowell said.

"Thanks, but no. I'll be fine."

"I heard that we may get our first snowfall tonight or tomorrow," Lowell commented.

"Where'd you hear that? It's too warm to snow."

"Temperatures are supposed to drop."

"What are we going to do then, Lowell?" Tillie asked, quietly.

"I have a surprise for you," Lowell told her, grinning from ear to ear.

Tillie looked at him, wondering what he was up to now. She loved being with him, never knowing what he had up his sleeve.

He bent sideways, reached into his back pocket, and pulled out his wallet. "I got my driver's license renewed," he told her, looking like the cat that swallowed the canary.

"Why would. . ."

"Wait," he interrupted. "There's more."

"What?" Tillie asked, excited.

"I've had my car serviced and it's ready to go. From now on, we drive in a nice warm car when we go out. We can put Red and Blue inside for the winter. No more worries about snowy, slippery sidewalks to contend with."

"No way! Lowell, this is wonderful. You know, I've been so concerned about how we were going to get around after the weather got bad. Oh, this is great. I'm so happy I could kiss you."

"I can't wait for that kiss."

"And, you'll get it, as soon as I get up off this couch," Tillie said. "Oh, this is going to. . ." She hesitated and gave him a mischievous look.

"I know that look. What devilish thought did you just have?"

"Rosemary is going to have a fit when I tell her that you're driving your car again."

"Don't tell her," Lowell exclaimed. "She won't allow you to ride with me."

"She can't stop me and she can't have me committed. I'm still of sound mind, you know, no matter what my daughter thinks," Tillie said grinning. "At least, most of the time," she added.

"So, what are you going to do?" Lowell asked.

"I know I have to tell her, but I won't tell her yet," Tillie said.

"What's going on in that head of yours?"

"How would you like to come to lunch on Sunday?" Tillie asked him.

It only took a second for her question to sink in and for Lowell to understand what she was getting at. "You are going to drive your daughter crazy," he said, grinning.

"She already is."

"No, she's not. She just has her hands full, that's all."

"You mean with me, don't you?" Tillie said.

"You can be a handful," Lowell told her.

"Sunday will be so much fun," Tillie declared. "I think everyone will be there. Well, maybe not Stacy's husband and kids. They hardly ever come to lunch anymore. I don't know why they have school sporting events on Sundays. Just doesn't seem right, somehow."

"I know. It's amazing how things have changed over the years," Lowell agreed. "I gather that lunch is still at one o'clock," he stated.

"It is. And, don't be late."

"Don't worry. I'll be there on time."

"Don't drive the car there, either," Tillie instructed. "If they see you with the car, it will ruin the surprise."

"I know," Lowell replied. "I will either walk or ride Blue. It depends on the weather."

"It's nice that we live so close to each other. How did we ever manage that?"

"It was fate. We were meant to be together."

Tillie smiled. "I think we were, too."

"It's only three-thirty. I think it's time I collect that kiss you promised me," he said, playfully.

Tillie smiled. "You do, do you? But, are you sure that you can . . .?" She glanced at Lowell's lap and grinned. "I guess you are."

"I took a Viagra after we ate, just in case," he told her. "Looks like it worked."

"There's no doubt about it," Tillie said, giggling. "Blue is definitely your color."

Tillie drove Red up the ramp onto the front porch and hit the doorbell. She hummed, *It's Been a Long, Long Time*, while she waited for her daughter to answer the door. Annoyed at being kept out in the cold, she pushed the button again.

"Is there any reason you can't open the door by

yourself?" Rosemary called out, as she came up the steps onto the porch.

"I forgot my key," Tillie told her. "Where were you?"

"In back, covering the roses. I heard it might snow tonight."

"I know. Lowell mentioned it."

"The door is unlocked," Rosemary said. "You can go in."

"Oh," Tillie said, surprised. "Since when do you keep the doors unlocked?"

"I saw your key on the table and figured you'd be home soon. I unlocked the door so you could get in."

"Oh. Sorry, I bothered you, then." Tillie got off of her scooter and pushed open the front door. "After you, Rosemary," she said. She climbed back onto Red and followed her daughter into the house.

"Your tires are dirty, Mother. I wish you wouldn't ride that thing in the house."

"I'm sorry, dear, but I'm not going to keep it outside. Anyway, Red will be put away soon so he can hibernate over the winter."

Rosemary turned and looked at her mother, wondering if she had heard right. "You're going to store him for the winter?" she asked.

"Of course, dear. You don't think I would ride him in the snow, do you?"

Rosemary stared at her, trying to figure out if she was serious. "No, of course not," she said after a few moments, not sure why her mother was being so reasonable.

Tillie took off her coat and hung it up. "Are we

having anything special for lunch on Sunday?"

"I don't know what I'm going to fix yet. Why?" Rosemary asked her.

"I asked Lowell to come."

"That's fine. He knows what time, doesn't he?"

"Of course, he does. He's been here before, you know."

"I know," Rosemary replied. "But I think you should remind him, just in case he forgot."

Tillie let out a deep sigh. "He's not senile. He knows what time to be here."

"Good. Your grandchildren know, too, but they never seem to manage to get here on time. Maybe, they're the ones who need reminding and not you old farts," Rosemary said, teasing her mother.

"Make fun, if you want, but you aren't that far behind us," Tillie said, smiling.

"Ain't that the truth?" Rosemary declared.

Nine

"I don't understand how you can eat that," Stacy said, turning up her nose. "That was a living thing once, you know."

"Stacy Elizabeth, you knock it off, right now!" her father practically shouted. "If you want to eat nothing but weeds, be my guest, but you keep your comments to yourself. Your mother works hard to put a nice meal on this table and I won't have you ruining it."

"Wow, you did it now," Lynn said. "Dad just called you Stacy Elizabeth. He must really be mad at you."

"That's enough out of you, too, young lady," Joseph said.

Joseph looked over at Lowell and smiled. "Sorry for the outburst, Lowell. Lunch isn't usually so lively."

"No problem." He glanced over at Rosemary. "This meal is delicious, Rosemary. You are one lucky man, Joseph, to have a woman who can cook like this," Lowell declared.

"I taught her everything she knows," Tillie said proudly. "Didn't I, Rosemary?"

"What's that, Mother?" Rosemary said.

"I taught you how to cook, didn't I?" Tillie looked at Lowell. "From the time she was old enough to stand on a stool in the kitchen, she watched me cook. As soon as she was old enough, she wanted to get her fat little hands in the dough and bake bread. All in all, I'd say she turned out pretty well in the kitchen department."

Rosemary smiled at the compliment. "Why, thank you, Mother. I appreciate that."

"Of course," Tillie continued, "there are a few other departments that she could use some help with." She stabbed a piece of pot roast with her fork and started to put it in her mouth. She glanced over at Lowell, who was watching her, and smiled. He gave her a slight nod and continued to eat.

"What departments are you referring to?" Rosemary asked her, obviously a little upset.

"Not important, Dear," Tillie said. She looked at Junior and smiled.

"What?" Junior asked, suddenly feeling ill at ease.

"I was wondering if there is anything I need to do to Red before I put him in storage for the winter months?"

"Well, I don't. . . I mean I've never. . . I'm not really sure." Junior looked at his father. "Dad, this is more your area of expertise. Perhaps, you could tell grandma what she needs to do."

Lynn looked surprised. "I didn't think you'd let Red out of your sight."

"Don't you ever use it in the house?" Stacy commented.

"Red, Stacy. His name is Red, not it," Tillie told her.

"Sorry, Grandma. I thought you used Red in the house, too. Not just outside."

"Well, I don't. It seems I fall down more outside than inside, so I don't need to use him in here." She ate a forkful of potatoes and stared at Joseph. "Well?"

72

she said, as she swallowed.

Joseph looked across the table at her and shrugged. "I have no idea. It's an electric scooter, so I don't think you have to do anything. You can put him in the shed out back, I guess."

"Oh, no," Tillie said. "Lowell has room in his garage, which is attached to his house. Plus, his garage is heated, so Red will be nice and cozy this winter. I just wondered if there was anything special I had to do."

"I think you're good," Joseph said. "If you want, I'll check the manual that came with it to be sure. However, if you are going to store him in Lowell's heated garage, I'm pretty sure you don't have to do anything."

"Thank you, Joseph," Tillie said.

"You have a scooter, Lowell," Joseph stated. "Does that sound about right to you?"

"Sounds good to me," Lowell said. "Lynn, could you pass me the rolls, please."

"Lowell has a big garage, you know," Tillie declared.

"Yes, Mother, we know. We've driven by his house lots of times."

"He only keeps one car in it, so there is plenty of room for Red and Blue," Tillie added.

Junior looked over at his grandmother. "Blue? What's blue?"

"Blue, dear. With a capital B. That's the name of Lowell's scooter," Tillie told him.

"That's right. I forgot about that," Junior said, grinning. "Red and Blue. Is there a White, too?"

"Why would there be a white?" Tillie asked. "That's just plain dumb."

"Well, Grandma, I think it's great that you aren't going to try to ride Red outside this winter. Riding on snow and ice could be dangerous. Good for you," Lynn exclaimed.

"Oh, we know better than to do that, don't we Lowell?" Tillie said as she patted Lowell's hand. "Besides, there's no reason to now, seeing as how Lowell got his driver's license renewed."

"That's right, Tillie," Lowell said, smiling at her.

"He what?" Rosemary asked, her voice barely a whisper.

"He renewed his driver's license. He passed the test with flying colors. I'm so proud of him. From now on, we'll be tooling around in his big warm car. Right, sweetie?" Tillie said, grinning.

"That's right," Lowell answered. "I wonder if you'd mind passing the potatoes, Junior? I could go for another helping."

"I swear, Rosemary, this man just never gets full. All he does, all day long, is eat."

"Now, Tillie, you know there's a few other things I do besides eat," Lowell said, his arm outstretched, still waiting for Junior to pass the potatoes.

"He's legal, Rosemary. You can't stop him from driving."

"For god's sake, Joseph, he's eighty years old. I can't have my mother riding in a car with him."

"Well, I'd rather see her in a car than riding around on that damned scooter. At least, she has some metal around her to protect her in case of an accident."

Rosemary threw the kitchen towel down on the counter and stepped away from the sink. "She's driving me crazy. Just when I think everything is okay, she tosses another knife at me. I think we should put her in a home."

"No, you don't. You didn't mean that, Rosemary," Joseph said. He pulled a chair away from the table and sat down. "Come here," he said, reaching out for Rosemary. He took her hand and pulled her onto his lap.

"You're right. I didn't mean it," Rosemary said, tears rolling down her cheeks. "I just get so upset with her."

"I know," he said, wiping a tear off of her face. "You know she does these things just to get your goat."

"But, why? Sometimes, I think she hates me."

"No, she doesn't hate you. You just have to learn not to let her bother you so much."

Rosemary wiped the corner of her eye with her apron. "That's a lot easier said than done."

"I know. I have to admit, though, I didn't see this one coming. The two of them played it beautifully," Joseph said, chuckling.

Rosemary jumped up off Joseph's lap. "You think this is funny?"

"I think that Lowell is the best thing that has happened to your mother since your dad died. So, what, if they play a little game now and then? They haven't got a whole lot of years left and I'm glad that she's happy."

Rosemary stared at her husband for a moment and started to walk out of the room. She turned and looked back at him. "I can't do this anymore, Joseph. I'm going to start looking into retirement homes."

"Come on, Rosemary. You're overreacting."

"Maybe, I am. But tomorrow I start checking them out."

"What are you doing down there?" Stacy asked, seeing her grandmother on her hands and knees, half under the dining room table.

"I lost an earring. I thought it might be down here."

"Get up. I'll look for it," Stacy said.

"Here you are, you little devil," Tillie said, as she pulled off her right earring and backed out from under the table. She held up her hand, so Stacy could see it.

"Let me help you up," Stacy said, taking her grandmother's arm.

"Thank you, dear," Tillie said, as she stood up. "Tell me, Stacy, do you think I'm senile?"

Stacy laughed. "Are you kidding? You're the sharpest old woman I know. Believe me, Grandma, you have a long way to go before you will even be close to senile." She looked at Tillie's face, realizing that her grandmother was serious. "What made you ask that?"

"So, you don't think I'm ready for an old fart's home?"

"What in the world. . . Of course not. Why would you even think that?"

"Your mother thinks I am."

Stacy put her arms around her grandmother

76

and hugged her. "I'll fight anybody who even thinks about putting you in a home," she whispered. "You ain't going anywhere, old lady."

T en

"Are you going somewhere?" Rosemary inquired.

Tillie, who was bundled up in her winter coat, scarf, and gloves, shook her head no.

"Then, why are you sitting here in the hallway with your coat on?"

"I'm waiting for Lowell to pick me up."

"You just said you weren't going anywhere." Rosemary stared at her mother. "Is that your suitcase you're sitting on?"

"It is," Tillie replied.

"So, you're bundled up in your coat, sitting on a suitcase, waiting for Lowell, but you're not going anywhere. Do I have that right?"

"I'm only going to his house, so I'm not really going anywhere. I'll only be a few blocks away."

"Why are you sitting on your suitcase?" Rosemary asked.

Tillie sighed. "I'm taking some of my things over there, that's all. Please, Rosemary, don't make a big deal out of this."

"What kind of things?" Rosemary inquired. "I'm just curious, that's all."

Tillie looked up at her daughter. "I'm spending a lot of time there and . . ."

"You're right about that," Rosemary interrupted. "You're at his house more than here."

"Anyway, as I was saying, we thought it would be a good idea if I had a change of clothes there. And, maybe a nightie and robe, in case I decide to spend the night."

Rosemary looked surprised. "Do you think that's a good idea, Mother? I mean, what if the neighbors see you? There's bound to be talk."

Tillie laughed. "So, let them talk. God, you are such a prude."

"I am not a prude. Seriously, what do you think you're doing? And, at your age." She shook her head back and forth.

"What month is this, Rosemary?"

Rosemary looked confused by the question. "Why?"

"Just tell me. What month is this?"

"It's October," Rosemary said.

"It's almost the end of October. And, it's winter. Right?" Tillie said, patiently.

"Obviously," Rosemary replied, getting irritated.

"And, we've already had a couple of snowfalls. Right?"

"Right."

"So, if I'm at Lowell's and it snows or the roads are icy, I'll stay there rather than have him drive me home. And, if I stay there, I'll need something to sleep in and some clean underwear. And, that's why I'm taking a suitcase of clothes to his house. Although, I guess I could sleep in the nude and I wouldn't need the nightie. But I'd like to take some clean panties and a bra with me. What do you think, Rosemary?"

Rosemary stared her mother in the eyes, trying hard to control her temper. "I think, maybe, you should pack up everything you own and take it with you to Lowell's. Maybe, you should just stay there and not bother to come back here at all."

Tillie broke eye contact with her daughter and looked away. "Is that how you really feel?" she asked, in a soft voice.

Rosemary covered her mouth with her hands, shocked at what she had just said. "I'm sorry, Mother. I didn't mean that. That was a horrible thing to say. Please, forgive me."

"It's all right. I know I can be difficult at times. Maybe, I should stay there. You could have the house all to yourself without me being underfoot."

"No, that's not what I meant. Please, stop it. I'm sorry."

"And, you could build a nice fire in the fireplace, and burn all those brochures. Did you decide which home you were going to dump me in, yet? I understand that Beaver Dam has a few places that don't cost a lot and I'd be close to Junior there. Maybe, he'd come and visit me once a month or so. Until, he got tired of it, of course. And, then, I'll just sit and look out a window, hoping that someone in my family remembers that I'm not dead yet."

Rosemary jumped, as the doorbell rang, scaring her.

"I'll get that," Tillie told her. "It's probably Lowell."

An hour later, Tillie and Lowell were sitting on his couch, enjoying a warm fire and drinking hot chocolate. "I love my daughter with all my heart," Tillie said, "but, the last six months have been hell. It seems that all we do is fight."

"It's been going on ever since you got Red.

80

Right?" Lowell asked.

"I guess. That seems about right."

"Well, I, for one, am glad you got him. If you hadn't ridden him to the Dairy Queen that day, we probably wouldn't be together now. And, I think hooking up with you is the best thing that's happened to me in years. I wouldn't change what we've got for anything."

"You realize that she's been checking out old people's homes, don't you? It's only a matter of time before she tosses me into one."

"I'll never let that happen. You can always live here with me, you know," Lowell told her.

Tillie looked over at him and smiled. "You are the sweetest man," she said. "I'm so glad you're in my life."

"I mean it, Tillie." Lowell took her hand. "How about we get married?"

Tillie's mouth dropped open in surprise. "You're not serious," she asked.

"Why not? We get along. We enjoy the same things. You're here most of the time, anyway. And, if we were married, Rosemary would have no say over you and couldn't dump you in a home someplace."

Tillie grinned. "You are serious."

"Of course, I am. What do you say? Are you game?"

"Well, we do have fun together and the. . ."

"And, the what?" Lowell prompted.

"The sex is good," Tillie said.

"It's the best," Lowell agreed. "Although, I might slow down a little as I get older."

"That's okay. I probably will, too."

Lowell slid off the couch and knelt down in front of her. "Ow," he exclaimed. "Damn knees."

"What are you doing?" Tillie said, laughing. "You know you're never going to be able to get up."

Lowell took Tillie's right hand and smiled. "Matilda Weiner, will you marry me? I'm sorry I don't have a ring, but we can get one later."

"I don't need a ring, Lowell. Save your money. I probably couldn't get one on my finger, anyway, with my knuckles so swollen."

"But we should have rings for the ceremony, shouldn't we?"

"I'll figure something out," Tillie declared, smiling.

"Then, it's a yes?" Lowell asked.

"It's a yes."

"One more thing," Lowell said.

"What's that?"

"Can you help me up, please?"

Eleven

"I wonder who that could be," Rosemary commented, as the doorbell rang. She grabbed a kitchen towel, drying her hands as she walked to the door.

"I'll get it," Tillie called out, as she came running down the stairs.

"Slow down before you trip and fall," Rosemary yelled. She opened the door and saw Lowell standing on the front porch. "Oh. It's Lowell," she said.

"Well, let him in," Tillie ordered. "It's freezing outside."

"Come on in, Lowell," Rosemary said, as she swung the front door open.

"Morning," Lowell said, as he entered the house. He glanced at his watch. "Whoops. It's after twelve. I guess I should have said good afternoon, Rosemary."

"Mother didn't tell me you were coming over. Are you staying for lunch?"

"I'd love to, if there's enough to go around," Lowell said, smiling.

Tillie took his coat and hung it on a hook. "We always have enough, don't we, Rosemary? We've been so blessed."

"Joseph's watching TV if you care to join him in the living room. Some game or pre-game something or other. I can't keep up with it all," Rosemary said. "Mother, would you like to help me in the kitchen?"

"I'll just set an extra plate first," Tillie told her.

"Well, look at that," Joseph exclaimed, as he looked out the window. "Stacy and the kids are here already."

"Is Simon with her?" Rosemary asked.

"Don't think so. Nope. Don't see him."

"I swear, it's been so long since I've seen him, I'm beginning to wonder if they are still married," Rosemary muttered, as she walked into the kitchen.

"That meal was fantastic," Lowell declared. "I think I'm going to miss these Sunday lunches."

Rosemary's head jerked up and she looked at Tillie. "What does Lowell mean, Mother? Is he going somewhere?"

Tillie smiled. "Ask Lowell."

All eyes went to Lowell, as they waited for him to explain his comment. He reached over and took Tillie's hand. He smiled, obviously happy, as he looked at everyone seated at the table. "Tillie and I have been thinking about spending a few months in Florida. I've got family down there and we will probably stay with them."

"Is that right, Mother? Do you plan on being gone for the rest of the winter?"

"I do. And, after we get back, Lowell and I are going to get married. It will probably be in early summer. Isn't that right, Sweetie?"

Lynn, who was taking a sip of water, coughed so hard that the water in her mouth went flying across the table, some of it hitting Junior in the face. "What the hell, Lynn," he yelled, as he wiped off the water with his napkin.

"Sorry," she sputtered.

Lowell looked over at Rosemary, smiling a huge

smile. "I can't tell you how happy I am. Never in a million years did I think I'd find happiness again. Tillie is. . ." His voice broke and tears filled his eyes. "Sorry," he mumbled, as he wiped his eyes with his napkin. "It's just that I'm so damn happy."

Lynn jumped out of her chair and ran to her grandmother and hugged her. "I'm so happy for you both." She turned and looked at her father. "Dad, do you have a bottle of wine you can open so we can toast Grandma and Lowell?"

"Well, I'm not sure." He looked at Rosemary. "Do we have any wine?" he asked her.

Rosemary stared at Tillie, not saying anything.

"Mom, are you okay?" Stacy asked.

"I think I left something on the stove," Rosemary said, as she left the table and walked into the kitchen.

"I should have expected that," Tillie commented. "I don't know why I thought she'd be happy for us. Perhaps, it would be best if Lowell and I leave now."

"No," Joseph exclaimed. "We're going to have that toast. This is good news and I'm happy for both of you. We all are, aren't we kids?"

"I know I am," Stacy replied.

"Me, too," Lynn declared.

"Junior," Joseph said. "Go downstairs and bring up a bottle of wine. I'm pretty sure there's a bottle or two still down there. Stacy, get some glasses and, Lynn, you go get the bottle opener. We're going to celebrate Tillie's and Lowell's engagement."

"And, have dessert," Lynn added.

"That goes without saying," Joseph said.

"Joseph?" Rosemary said, quietly.

Stacy glanced over at her mother, who was standing in the doorway. "Mom, are you okay?"

"I think I'm having a heart attack. Would you call 911?"

"Junior, call. . ."

"I'm on it," Junior told his father, reaching for his phone.

Tillie stared at her daughter for a few moments. "There's nothing wrong with her," she declared. "She just can't stand the fact that I'm happy."

"Grandma, I don't think Mom is faking this," Lynn stated.

"We'll see," Tillie muttered. "We'll see."

"I'm okay," Rosemary told Lynn, as she took off her coat.

Lynn looked over at her dad. "Is she okay?"

"She's fine," Joseph said. "It wasn't a heart attack."

"Well, what happened, then? She certainly didn't look fine when she left here four hours ago."

"I said I'm fine, Lynn. It was nothing. Just drop it, will you?" Rosemary said.

"Dad?" Lynn asked, looking at her father.

"It was an anxiety attack, brought on by your grandmother's news about her and Lowell. Your mother just has to take it easy for a few days."

"That's it?" Lynn inquired. She blew out a deep breath and smiled. "Well, thank goodness for that. I can't tell you how worried I was."

Joseph looked around the living room. "Where's everyone?"

"They went home. Stacy had to get the kids to some party or something. I told her I'd call her as soon as I heard something about mom. By the way, Dad, I would have appreciated a phone call letting us know how mom was doing. I've been sitting on pins and needles, worried about her."

"I didn't have my phone with me. If it had been anything serious, I would have called you on a hospital phone," Joseph told his daughter.

"Where's your grandmother?" Rosemary asked Lynn.

"She left with Lowell. They went back to his place."

"She just left, without even knowing how I was doing. How could she do that?" Rosemary asked.

"She was afraid to be here when you got home," Lynn said. "I'll give her a call and let her know that you're okay."

Rosemary looked surprised. "Why would she be afraid to be here?"

"Grandma was upset, Mother. She thinks what happened to you was her fault and she didn't want to upset you again. She feels really, really bad about it."

Rosemary stared at Lynn for a moment. "Well, she should feel bad and it was her fault," she said angrily.

"Come on, Mom. I'm sure she didn't mean for this to happen to you," Lynn said. "She just wanted to surprise everyone."

"Oh, she did, did she? Well, I didn't think she could do much more to surprise me, but this takes the cake. I'm done pretending, Lynn. Your grandmother is driving me to an early grave with all her nonsense. It isn't bad enough that she's carrying on like a slut with that man. Now they want to get married? What is wrong with those two?"

"Mother!" Lynn exclaimed. "That's pretty strong language. How can you call grandma a slut?"

"Well, what would you call her? Sleeping over at his house, not caring what the neighbors think. She's acting like a. . ."

"Perhaps, it's time to take another pill," Joseph interrupted, worried about Rosemary's stress level.

"What pill?" Lynn asked her dad.

"It's to calm her down." He pulled a small bottle out of his pocket and looked at the label. "It's Valium. The doctor said it's for her nerves. That's just for now, though. I have a couple more prescriptions for her that I'll get filled in the morning."

"What are they?" Lynn asked, showing concern.

Joseph reached into his pocket and pulled out two pieces of paper. He handed them to Lynn. "Here, you tell me. I don't know anything about drugs."

Lynn looked at the two prescriptions, trying to decipher the doctor's handwriting. "What did he say about the Valium?" she asked her father.

"He said that she should take them tonight and in the morning. I think he only gave her eight pills."

"There's a prescription for Xanax," Lynn said, reading from one of the pieces of paper. "That would be to calm her down." She looked at the second piece of paper. "This one is for Ambien."

"What does that do?" Joseph asked her.

"It will help her sleep," Lynn told him. "Basically,

she'll be like a zombie during the day and she'll be out at night." She looked at her dad and frowned. "I don't like this. Mom shouldn't be taking all these drugs. Did the doctor say anything else?"

"He wants to see her in five days. To see if she's better – you know – calmer. If she is, he'll have her stop the pills."

"I don't know, Dad. I don't like the idea of mom taking this crap."

"It's only for a few days, Lynn. She needs some rest and this might be the way for her to get it. Besides, I could use a good night's sleep, too. Maybe, I'll take a few of those Ambius pills, too."

"Dad!" Lynn exclaimed.

"Just kidding," Joseph said grinning.

"And, they're called Ambien, not Ambius. Where's mom?" Lynn asked, looking around the living room.

"I think she went upstairs to bed," Joseph said. "I think you should probably leave now. You've got a long drive."

"It's only about forty-five minutes, Dad. I'll be fine." She looked over at her father, thinking that he was certainly showing his age tonight. "Would you like me to stay? I could take care of mom and you could get some sleep."

"My little Lynn. Always ready to step up and take care of people. But, no. We're fine. You go, now. We'll be fine."

"You sure?"

"Go, will you?" Joseph said. "I'll call you in the morning."

"Are you at home?" Stacy asked.

"Yeah. I got here a few minutes ago. I called Junior and clued him in."

"How's mom?"

"She's fine," Lynn said. "It was just an anxiety attack."

"God, Lynn, Mom scared the hell out of me. I just don't get why she is so upset about Grandma and Lowell. You would think she'd be happy for her," Stacy said.

"This all started with that damn scooter, you know. Since that day, it seems that all they have done is fight. I think mom hates to admit that grandma doesn't need her to take care of her. It kind of gave mom a purpose and, now that she realizes she isn't needed, she's angry. I kind of feel sorry for her." Lynn reached for her beer and took a long swallow. "Grandma is going to move into Lowell's house permanently now. She doesn't think it's a good idea to stay with mom and dad any longer. She asked if I would help her move her stuff."

"It is her house. She doesn't have to move out if she doesn't want to. I wonder what she'll do with it after she moves," Stacy said.

"Do with what?" Lynn inquired.

"The house. Do you think she'll sell it?"

"Of course not. Where would mom and dad live if she did that?" Lynn asked.

"Good question. You know, it might be a good idea if mom thought about that and cooled it. What else did grandma say?" Stacy asked.

"That this doesn't change anything and they are still going to get married and go on a cruise for their honeymoon. It sounds like Lowell has already booked it." Lynn laughed.

"What's so funny?" Stacy asked.

"They're having sex," Lynn told her. "Grandma said it was great."

"OMG!" Stacy yelled. "You have got to be friggin' kidding me."

"I'm serious. Grandma told me. Maybe that's why mom's so upset," Lynn said. "Maybe dad can't get it up anymore and she's jealous that grandma is getting laid and she isn't."

"Hold on," Stacy said.

Lynn took another swallow of beer, waiting for Stacy to come back to her phone.

"Lynn?"

"I'm here," Lynn said.

"I've got to go. Lisa has her finger caught in the tub faucet."

Lynn held back a laugh. "Okay. I'll talk to you later. Go take care of Lisa. Love ya. Bye."

"Love you, too. Bye."

RED . . . . Susan L Pare'

April, 2018

Twelve

"Are you sure they're coming home today?" Lynn asked her sister.

"Absolutely. Grandma called me last night. They are flying into O'Hare and from there they will catch a connecting flight to Madison. I'm picking them up there around three-thirty," Stacy said.

"They were sure gone a long time. I never expected Grandma to be gone over Christmas and Easter."

"It's probably for the best. Mom is the happiest I've seen her in a long time. I really think that this has helped their relationship. Grandma told me that she talks to Mom a couple of times a week. Considering that they weren't talking at all when she left, that's real progress," Stacy said.

"Let me know when they're home, will you?" Lynn asked.

"Of course."

"By the way, is Grandma going to her house or to Lowell's house?"

"I haven't a clue, but I'll let you know."

"What do you mean they weren't on the flight?" Lynn shouted. "Where the hell are they?"

"Stop yelling, will you? I just told you I don't know where they are and neither does the airline. They said that they never got on the plane at O'Hare."

"What the hell, Stacy? Wait. Let me think a minute."

Stacy waited for a few seconds, waiting for her

sister to talk. "Well?" she finally blurted out. "Are you done thinking yet?"

"First of all, did you try calling Grandma's cell phone?"

"Of course. That's the first thing I did."

"What about Lowell's phone? Did you try that?"

"I've been trying each phone every few minutes, but they don't answer. Their phones just ring and ring," Stacy told her.

"Okay. Do you have their itinerary? Do you know what flight they took to O'Hare from Florida?"

"I have it in my purse. Hang on a sec."

Lynn waited impatiently for Stacy to dig the information out of her purse. "Did you find it?" she finally yelled into her phone.

"Hold on. Okay, I've got it. They flew American, Flight #267."

"All right," Lynn said. "You need to call American Airlines and see if they were on the flight. Tell them it's an emergency – anything – but make them tell you."

"I could use you here, Lynn. I don't know why Grandma didn't ask you to pick them up. After all, you don't live far from the airport."

"How should I know why? Who knows what goes on in that old woman's head?" Lynn replied. "Do you have the number for American?"

"I've got it right here."

"Then, call them and find out what the hell happened to those two, will you? And, call me right back."

"I don't understand why you don't just drive over here."

Lynn sighed. "Just call them."

Stacy stared at her phone. "Lynn?" she shouted and then realized that her sister had hung up on her.

An hour and ten minutes later, after much pleading, crying, threatening, and more pleading, Stacy finally talked to a representative at American Airlines. She told them that Tillie and Lowell had debarked the plane at O'Hare and, other than the fact that they had a smooth flight, there was no other information they could give her.

Stacy speed-dialed Lynn and waited for her to answer her cell phone.

"What?" Lynn yelled as she answered her phone.

"They're missing, Lynn. They got off the plane in Chicago, and that's all anyone knows. There is a possibility that they missed their flight to Madison. Airport security is checking all the terminals between where they got off the plane and where they should have boarded the plane to Madison. They might just be wandering around. We're staying in touch."

"Shit. We've lost our Grandmother again," Lynn said, laughing.

"What's so funny? This isn't funny," Stacy said, starting to get angry.

"Are you crying?" Lynn asked her.

"Of course, I'm crying. My grandmother is missing, for cripes sake. And, you think it's funny."

"Well, it kinda is," Lynn uttered. "I mean, isn't that kinda what she does? Goes missing, I mean. And, she always turns up, Stacy. So, quit crying, will you?"

"I just don't. . . I've got another call. I'll call you

back."

"You are not going to believe this," Stacy exclaimed when Lynn answered her phone.

"What?"

"I've just talked to the agent from United and he said . . ."

"Why United?" Lynn interrupted.

"That's the airlines they were flying on from O'Hare to Madison. It seems that Grandma and Lowell took their scooters with them to Florida. Did you know the airlines have to fly wheelchairs and mobility scooters free?

"Really? I didn't know that," Lynn uttered.

"Anyway, he told me that their scooters are here ready to be picked up in the luggage area." Stacy took a deep breath and let it out. "Lynn? Are you there?"

Lynn covered the phone with her hand, laughing so hard she was shaking.

"Lynn! Did you hang up? You better not have hung up on me."

Lynn, still trying to control her laughter, coughed loudly. "Sorry. I seem to have swallowed the wrong way."

"You're laughing, aren't you?" Stacy asked. "You think this is soo funny."

"For god's sake, Stacy, loosen up a little, will you? I'm sorry, but this is so Grandma. I'll be there in a few minutes. Where are you?"

"It's about time you got your butt over here and helped me. I'm at United Terminal 5."

"All right. In the meanwhile, stay in touch with

the agents that are trying to find those two idiots."

Stacy jumped out of her chair when she saw her sister coming towards her. "They found them," she cried out, starting to cry.

"It's all right," Lynn told her as she gave her a big hug. "It's gonna be okay."

Stacy took a step back and looked her sister in the eyes. "You think so, do you? Do you know what those two. . . What did you call them? Oh, yeah. Do you know what those two idiots did?"

"Let's sit for a minute," Lynn said, as she took Stacy's hand and walked over to the seats.

Stacy wiped her eyes with the back of her hand and sat down.

"Breathe, Stacy. My god, I don't think I've ever seen you this upset."

"Well, I have a good reason, don't you think?" she snapped at her sister.

Lynn glanced around at her surroundings and smiled. "There's a bar over there. You want to go get a drink?"

"What in the world is. . ." She turned and looked over at the bar and smiled. "Why the hell not? Let's go."

"It seems Lowell decided that he should rent a truck so he could take the scooters home." She took a sip of her drink and sighed. "God, I needed that."

"But I don't understand why he would do that," Lynn declared.

"He didn't quite understand that the scooters

99

would be transferred from American to United. He thought they would be left in Chicago, so he decided he would rent a U-Haul and drive home."

Lynn stared at her sister. "You're kidding me."

"Swear to god, Sis. He was planning on driving all the way from O'Hare Airport to Columbus. The only problem was – now get this – after he rented the truck, he couldn't find the scooters. Of course, the scooters were on the plane to Madison by that time."

Lynn grinned. "My god, Stacy, you can't make this shit up. Where are they now?"

"Wait. So, the next thing you know, Lowell is reporting the theft of the two scooters to the cops. The U-Haul people are waiting to take him to get the truck and the cops want to take him and Grandma to the Police Department located at O-Hare to sign a complaint."

"There's a Police Department at O-Hare?"

"There is," Stacy told her. "Then, Grandma starts ranting about how Red and Blue went missing and gets everyone confused. The cops think that a couple of dogs or cats have gone missing or been stolen. Finally, they sit down with the agent from United and get the whole story. Anyway, the cops send the U-Haul guy trucking, telling him that a truck isn't needed and the agent from United calls me."

Lynn is biting the inside of her cheek, trying not to laugh. "Damn that Red," she mutters, making Stacy totally lose it. "So where . . . are they. . . now?" Lynn asks, barely able to talk.

"Idiot number one and idiot number two are being put on the next flight from O-Hare to Madison, courtesy of United Airlines," Stacy told her.

"When does that arrive?"

"If we're lucky and they don't lose them, Grandma and Lowell should be here around nine-thirty tonight."

Lynn checked her watch. "Well, we might as well stay here. We could load up the scooters and their luggage while we're waiting."

"Do you think there will be enough room for them, the scooters, and their luggage in your SUV?" Lynn asked.

"I think so. If there isn't, you'll have to take them home in your car," Stacy said.

The two women finished their drinks.

"We've got a few hours to kill. One more?" Stacy asked.

"That's a plan."

Thirteen

The plane arrived on time, and a few minutes later Tillie, accompanied by an attendant who was pushing Lowell in a wheelchair, came through the door. Tillie grinned when she saw her two granddaughters standing in the terminal, waving at her.

"Grandma, you have no idea how good it is to see you. You had us worried there for a little while."

"Does your mother know what happened?" Tillie asked as she hugged Stacy.

"Not yet," Stacy said, smiling.

"Then, she won't know, because you two aren't going to tell her."

Lynn hugged her. "What if she asks why you arrived so late?"

"Just tell her we missed our connection and had to wait for a later plane. Got it?"

"Got it, Grams," Lynn said. She looked down at Lowell, who looked like he was asleep. "What's with him?"

Tillie shook her head. "Damn fool. He's drunk. He couldn't even get off the plane by himself."

Lynn grinned. "What the hell, Grams? How did that happen? Your flight was only a half-hour."

"That might be, but the wait to get on that damn plane was a hell of a lot longer. What can I say? They shouldn't have bars in airports and that limp dick sitting there is proof of that."

Stacy and Lynn stared at her, shocked at her language.

"Limp dick? Seriously Grams? I'm surprised at you."

"Oh, grow up, will you?" Tillie glanced around the terminal. "Are we ready to leave? I'd like to get home. I need a bath and I'm tired."

"I'm parked in front," Stacy told her. "In fact, a very nice security guard is watching the car for me, so I don't get a ticket for illegal parking. Everyone here at United wanted to be sure that you wouldn't be inconvenienced when you arrived." She looked at the attendant, who was still standing behind Lowell's wheelchair. "Do you want me to take him out?" she asked.

"No Ma'am. My instructions are to see that he is put safely into your car."

Lynn looked over at Stacy and smiled. "I can't even imagine what these people have had to put up with the past few hours."

"Probably afraid of a lawsuit," Stacy said.

"Are you kidding? It's Lowell and Tillie that should be afraid of one," Lynn told her.

Tillie looked at Lowell and shook her head. "I don't know what I ever saw in that man. I am so done with him."

The ringing of the doorbell woke Joseph and Rosemary. Rosemary glanced over at the clock on the nightstand and frowned. "It's eleven-thirty. Who in the world could that be?"

Joseph turned on a light and headed down the stairs to answer the door. He switched on the porch light and looked through the window. "What the hell?"

he muttered to himself. He opened the door and stared at his daughter. "Stacy? What's wrong?"

"I'm so sorry to wake you, Dad. Grandma is here. Can you throw on some clothes and help me bring in her luggage?"

"She's here? Just now? I thought she was home already. Her flight was at three-thirty."

"They missed that one and took a later flight. I need help getting her stuff out of the car."

Joseph glanced towards the car and saw Tillie walking towards the house. "Hi, Tillie. Did you have a nice vacation?"

"Vacation, my ass. It's good to be home. Help Stacy, will you? And, be careful when you take Red out of the car."

"Red? Why is Red here," Rosemary exclaimed from the doorway. "And, why aren't you staying at Lowell's? Are you moving back in?"

"I'll tell you tomorrow," Tillie said. "Right now, I'm tired and I'm going to bed." She brushed past her daughter and headed up the stairs to her bedroom.

"Stacy?"

"It's a long story, Dad. We can take the scooters out tomorrow. Just get Grandma's luggage, will you?"

"Scooters?" Rosemary said. "Why do you have scooters?"

"You might want to throw some pants on. We have to take Lowell home, too," Stacy told her dad.

"Why? Where's Lowell?" Joseph asked, looking confused.

"He's in the back seat, sleeping. Actually, he's drunk. I'll need help getting him into his house."

"Why is he drunk?" Rosemary cried out. "What is going on?"

"Mom," Stacy said softly. "I'll tell you all about it tomorrow. Right now, I just want to get Grandma's luggage out of the car and get Lowell home safe and sound. Is that okay with you? Please. I've had a rough night."

"Well, I'm sorry if. . ."

"Let me get some clothes on," Joseph interrupted. "Rosemary, why don't you put on a pot of coffee?"

"Coffee? At this time of night? You'll never get back to sleep."

"You're right. Then, how about making me a cup of hot chocolate? It shouldn't take long to get Lowell home and hot chocolate will probably taste pretty good when I get back here."

"Why don't you just say you want me to stay out of your way? I'm not stupid, you know," Rosemary snapped.

"Fine," Joseph said. He looked at Stacy and shrugged. "I'll be right back," he said and headed back into the house to put his pants on.

"Do you want to come in and have a cup of hot chocolate with me?" Joseph asked Stacy.

"Do you think Mom made hot chocolate?"

"Oh, yeah, she did. She's gonna want to know everything that happened and why Tillie is back here and not at Lowell's."

"I'd love to join you, Dad, but I'm pooped. Thanks for your help. There's no way I could have gotten Lowell into bed by myself. He was totally dead weight. Do you think he'll be okay by himself?"

"Probably. He's on his side, so if he does throw up he should be okay."

"Should be, but not for sure. Maybe, I should go back there and stay with him for a while. You know, just to be on the safe side," Stacy said.

"You go on home and get some sleep," Joseph told her. "Lowell will be fine."

"You sure?" she asked.

"I'm sure. Now go home."

"What time should I come over tomorrow, so we can unload those damn scooters?"

"Tomorrow's Sunday, Stacy."

"Oh, that's right. Sunday dinner. I'll be here around noon, then. Maybe, Simon will come tomorrow and he can help."

"One thing, before you leave," Joseph said, as he reached for the door handle.

"What's that, Dad?"

"Just why are those scooters in your car?"

Fourteen

"Are you still married to Simon?" Rosemary asked her daughter.

"Mother! Why in the world would you even ask me that? Of course, we're still married," Stacy told her.

"Well, I haven't seen him in months."

"He was here for Easter. You just don't remember, that's all."

"You're right. I'm getting senile," Rosemary declared.

"I didn't say that," Stacy responded. "Don't be putting words in my mouth." She studied her mother's face for a moment. "You're upset about something. What's the problem?"

"Seriously? You don't know? You drop your grandmother off in the middle of the night and now she's going to live here again and you don't know what the problem is?"

"She's only been here for less than a day. I don't know what you're so upset about."

"I'm sorry. I just haven't had time to adjust to her being back here, I guess," Rosemary said.

"Well, Mom, it is her house."

Rosemary gave her daughter a dirty look. "You don't need to remind me. I know it's her house."

"What's going on?" Lynn asked as she walked into the kitchen.

"Nothing," Rosemary said, as she started mashing the potatoes.

"Mom's upset because grandma is here," Stacy said.

Lynn put her arm around her mother and hugged her. "I know she can be difficult, Mom. I thought you two had gotten past your differences."

Rosemary wiped a tear from her eye. "We did. But I didn't know she was going to be living here again."

"Lynn, I'm going over to Lowell's to drop off his ride. How about coming along and helping me? Besides, I want to make sure he's okay. He wasn't feeling any pain last night and I'm sure he's got one hell of a headache."

"Let's go." Lynn took her mother's hand and squeezed it. "Mom, you know Grandma and Lowell just got into a fight. That's what couples do. They fight. There's a good chance that in a day or two they'll be back together again. I wouldn't sweat it if I were you. Just wait a little while and see what happens. Okay?"

Rosemary shook her head. "Okay. But you know how difficult. . ."

"Mom, just give it a chance," Stacy interrupted. She turned to Lynn and motioned that they should get going.

"These things aren't as heavy as I thought they were," Stacy said, as they unloaded Lowell's scooter from her van.

"You said that yesterday," Lynn told her.

"I know. And, now I said it again."

"You're turning into mom, you know. Always repeating things," Lynn said, grinning.

"I suppose we should put this in the garage so Lowell doesn't have to mess with it," Stacy said. "Go see if he's home and ask him to open the garage door."

Lynn went over to the back door and rang the bell. She waited, rang the bell again, and, then, knocked on the door. She turned and glanced back at Stacy. "There's no answer. Is his car in the garage?"

Stacy walked over to the garage and looked through a window. "It's here," he yelled.

"Do you have his phone number?" Lynn asked as she walked back to where Stacy was standing.

"I do. I'll call and see if he answers." She called Lowell's phone and waited. "It's ringing," she told Lynn.

"I'm gonna go listen at the door," Lynn said and ran to the back door. "I can hear it," she exclaimed. "He must be in there."

Lynn turned the door handle and opened the door. "It's open," she said and walked into the kitchen. "Lowell?" she yelled. "Lowell, it's Lynn. Are you okay?" She turned and looked at Stacy, who had followed her into the house. "I don't think he's here," she stated.

"Let's check the rest of the house," Stacy said. "He might still be asleep."

"He'd have to be dead to sleep through all the noise we're making," Lynn commented.

The sisters went through the living room and opened the door to Lowell's bedroom.

"I have a bad feeling about this," Lynn said. "By the way, did you leave the back door unlocked when you dropped him off last night?"

"I don't know. Dad shut the door. It might have been un . . . Oh, my god, Lynn."

"What is it?"

"I think he's dead," Stacy murmured.

Lynn glanced over at the bed. "Ooh, ick," she uttered. "It smells in here."

"Go see if he has a pulse," Stacy told her.

"You go. I'm not touching him. Besides, I'm pretty sure he's dead. Why else would he be laying half on and half off the bed?"

"There's blood by his head. Do you think he fell and hit his head?" Stacy asked her sister.

"He could have. I think he must have thrown up. His mouth is all white looking." Lynn shuddered. "I don't see any puke, though. God, Stacy, this really freaks me out."

"Oh, my god," Stacy suddenly cried out. "It's my fault. I never should have left him alone. I wanted to come back and stay with him, but dad said he'd be okay. If I'd come back here, he might still be alive." She started to cry.

"It's not your fault," Lynn said. "You didn't know this would happen. Besides, we don't know why he died. It could have been his heart or something."

"Oh, shit, oh, shit, oh shit!" Stacy exclaimed.

"What are you going on about now?"

"What about grandma, Lynn? How are we going to tell her? This is going to break her heart."

"Maybe," Lynn said. "She did say she was done with him, though, so maybe she won't be too upset."

"Of course, she's gonna be upset. She was just mad. She didn't mean it when she said they were through," Stacy said. She looked around the room and sighed. "I guess we need to call someone. Do we call his doctor or what?"

"Let's call dad. He'll know what to do," Lynn said.

"Good idea. Call him and tell him not to say anything to mom or grandma. Come on. Let's go into the other room. I don't want to stay in here."

As soon as they were in the living room, Lynn pulled her phone out of her back pocket and called her father.

"Lunch is ready," he whispered when he answered his phone. "Get your butts back here before your mother has a fit."

"Dad, stay calm and act like nothing is wrong. We need you to come over to Lowell's. He's dead. Don't tell anyone. Just say Stacy's car wouldn't start and you need to come help us. Okay?"

Joseph only hesitated for a second before he jumped out of his chair, grabbed his car keys off the small table in the entryway, and opened the door. "Girls need me," he yelled. "I'll be right back."

"What did your father say?" Rosemary asked Junior, as she walked into the living room.

"He'll be right back," Junior told her.

"Where is he going?"

"I don't know, Mom. He didn't say. Is lunch ready yet? I'm starving."

"Where's everyone?" Tillie asked, as she came down the stairs and looked into the living room. "I thought lunch was ready."

"It is," Rosemary said. "And, we're going to eat. I'm done putting up with this crap. Junior, help me put the food on the table. Mom, go sit down."

Tillie looked surprised. "We're going to eat

without Joseph and the girls?"

"We sure as high water are. Now, go sit down."

"It's all right to say hell, Rosemary. I've heard it before you know."

Fifteen

Joseph and his daughters were silent as they watched the ambulance back out of Lowell's driveway and head toward the funeral parlor.

Police Chief Daniel Austin and Officer Robert Gorski watched the vehicle until it was out of sight.

"Is there anything else we should do?" Joseph asked Austin.

"Well, his death is suspicious, so there will be an autopsy performed to determine the cause of death. I would like you and your daughters to come down to the station and write your statements. No big deal. Just that you found him and called me is enough, but I need it in writing."

"Right now?" Lynn asked.

"No, tomorrow is fine. I figure you need to be at home now with Tillie. Poor lady. I guess this is going to break her heart."

"Do you need all of us to make a statement?" Joseph asked.

"I do, Joe, if you don't mind."

"I'll come in after work tomorrow if that's okay."

"That's fine," Austin told him.

"Tillie has some of her stuff in Lowell's house. Is it all right if she gets it? I don't mean today, of course," Stacy said. "You know, when she's feeling better."

"Me or one of my officers will need to be with her when she decides to get it. She's not a blood relative, so she has no right to go in there without supervision."

Lynn looked over at Austin and shook her head in disgust. "For crying out loud, Dan, you act like she's

113

going to steal something or trash the place. They were going to get married in a few weeks. He gave her a key to the house. She was living here."

"Sorry, Lynn. Didn't mean it that way, but rules are rules. I'm asking you to keep her out, at least until the investigation is over. For now, I'm locking up the place."

"Can we put the scooters in the garage?" Stacy asked. "I don't think we should leave them out here on the driveway."

"Of course." He turned to Gorski and said, "Take care of that, will you?"

"I'm on it," Officer Gorski said.

"There's a button for the garage opener on the wall in the kitchen," Lynn told him.

"Thanks," Gorski replied.

"Come on, girls," Joseph said, "we need to go tell Tillie what happened."

"Wait," Lynn said loudly.

"What?" Gorski said, looking around.

"Grams is gonna want Red, Dad. Let's take her scooter back home with us."

"Where have you been?" Rosemary shouted. "Do you have any idea what time it is? Lunch was hours ago."

"I'm sorry. I should have called," Joseph replied. "Where's Tillie?"

"She's napping. We ate, you know. We decided we weren't going to wait for you, so we ate. What do you have to say about that?"

"Where's Junior?"

"He went home. Why?" Rosemary stared at Joseph, waiting for him to answer. "Something's wrong, isn't it?" she asked, after a few moments.

"I'm afraid so," Joseph said. "Lowell died sometime last night."

Rosemary shook her head. "What? That can't be right."

"I'm sorry. I didn't want to tell you on the phone. The police just left his house. The girls found him, and there were questions to answer. We had to call the doctor and there was stuff to take care. . ." Joseph's voice broke and he turned away so Rosemary wouldn't see him crying.

"Oh, my god," Rosemary cried out. "Mother's going to be devastated. How can I possibly tell her? Lynn, you do it. She likes you the best. It will be better if you tell her."

"I'm not telling her. She's your mother. You tell her."

"What do you mean, she likes Lynn the best? That's not a very nice thing to say," Stacy said, indignant at her mother's comment.

"Well, it's true," Rosemary said.

"Enough," Joseph yelled. "She likes you both equally. I'll tell her as soon as she wakes up. Satisfied?"

"I'm up. How could anyone sleep with all this commotion? So, what is it you have to tell me?" Tillie asked as she walked into the living room.

The room went quiet. Everyone looked down, inspecting their laps, waiting for someone to speak. Tillie stared at each of their faces and sighed. "Okay," she said softly. "Who died?"

Rosemary's head jerked up and she looked at her mother. "How did you know?"

"When you're as old as I am and have lost as many friends as I have, you recognize the death face. So, who was it?"

"I'm so sorry, Tillie," Joseph said. "Lowell passed away last night. The girls found him when they took his scooter over to his house a few hours ago."

Tillie stared at him. "Blue," she said after a few seconds.

"What?" Joseph said.

"His scooter's name was Blue," Tillie said softly. "What did he die from?"

"They're not sure. An autopsy has to be performed to determine the cause of death," Joseph told her.

"Damn old fool probably choked to death," Tillie said. "I'm sorry. He was a nice guy until he started drinking too much."

"I didn't know Lowell was a drinker," Lynn said.

"He wasn't before we went down to Florida. He started drinking a lot while we were there. You know, five o'clock cocktails starting at three o'clock. It got excessive after a while. He changed a lot. I was tempted to come home early, but I waited it out. I didn't feel right about leaving without him."

"Wow. That sure doesn't sound like the Lowell we knew," Stacy said.

"I know. I was beginning to think he might have a brain tumor or something. I was going to make him go see a doctor when we got back home."

"Well, I'm sorry, Tillie," Joseph said. "Are you okay?"

"Yeah, Grams, you don't seem very upset," Lynn commented.

"Lynn!" Rosemary shouted. "That's not a nice thing to say."

"That's okay, Rosemary," Tillie replied. "Everyone grieves in their own way, Lynn. I loved the man and I'm going to miss him, but I don't think I would have gone through with the wedding. He got too weird with the drinking and gambling and stuff. He wasn't the same anymore."

"Gambling, too?" Stacy said.

"He started playing the dogs and went to a lot of jai alai matches while we were there. He was losing a lot of money. I blame the people we were staying with. Lowell's cousin is a big gambler and he loves the casinos."

"I'm so sorry, Grandma," Stacy said, hugging her. "I know you have some of your things in Lowell's house. Chief Austin said you can get them anytime you want, but one of his men has to be with you."

"One thing at a time," Tillie said. "Let's get the man buried before we do anything. What funeral parlor is he at?"

"He has to be autopsied first, before the body is released for burial," Joseph said. "The coroner will pick him up from Jensen Funeral Parlor and then return him when they are finished."

Tillie sighed. "I'm going to go lay down." She reached out her hand to Lynn. "Help me get up, will you?"

"Do you want me to help you upstairs," Rosemary asked her.

"I'm fine," Tillie said, as she stood up. "I'll be just fine."

As she started up the stairs, she turned and looked at her family, who were watching her. "Where's Blue?" she asked.

"In Lowell's garage," Joseph told her. "He's safe."

"And, Red?"

"He's here, Tillie. We brought him home."

Sixteen

"Will you get that?" Rosemary yelled, from the kitchen.

Joseph laid his paper on the coffee table and went to answer the front door. "Chief Austin," he said, acknowledging the man, as he opened the front door. "I take it you have some news for us. Come on in."

"Thanks, Joe," Austin said as he entered the house. "I've got the results of the autopsy and thought I'd tell you in person, rather than call. Is Tillie home?"

"She is." Joseph stood at the bottom of the stairs and shouted, "Tillie, can you come down here, please?"

"What is it?" Tillie yelled back.

"Chief Austin is here. He'd like to talk to you."

"I'm coming."

"Please, sit down," Joseph said, motioning that Austin should have a seat in the living room.

"Nice weather we're having," Chief Austin declared, as he sat down on the couch.

"It sure is. Oh, Rosemary," Joseph said, as his wife walked into the room. "Daniel has some news for us."

"Really?" Rosemary said as she took a seat.

"The autopsy report," Joseph said.

Chief Austin started to stand, as Tillie came into the room. She motioned for him to stay seated. "Don't get up on my account," she told him. "So, what's the news? Did Lowell have a heart attack?"

Chief Austin reached into a pocket and pulled out an envelope. He took out a few sheets of paper, which were stapled together, and opened them. He glanced up at Joseph and Rosemary and frowned. "I'm afraid it isn't good news," he said. "Tillie, when was the last time you saw Lowell?"

Tillie looked confused. "I already told you that the last time I saw him was in the back seat of Stacy's car. He was asleep. Joseph and Stacy took him home and put him to bed."

"And, you didn't see him after that?" Austin inquired.

"No. I went to bed."

"What's going on, Dan?" Joseph asked. "Why are you asking Tillie these questions?"

"Lowell died sometime between three and four in the morning. The autopsy showed that he was murdered. I'm at the point now, in this investigation, where I have to make sure all the t's are crossed and the i's are dotted."

"Murdered!" Rosemary exclaimed. "Why would anyone want to murder Lowell?"

"That's what I intend to find out," Austin said. "A blow to the head is what killed him. It's possible that someone broke into the house to rob him and he woke up startling them, so they killed him. Tillie, would you know if anything was missing from his house?"

"I guess I would," Tillie replied. "Although, except for his coin collection, I don't think there was much in the house worth anything. I could look around, though, if you want me to."

"That would be helpful. Do you know anyone who might have a grudge against him? You know – would want to hurt him?"

Tillie shrugged. "Of course not. Everyone loved

Lowell."

"Well, whoever did it might have done him a favor. He would have been dead in a few days, anyway."

"What do you mean?" Joseph asked. "Was he sick? Tillie thought he had been acting strange for a while. Did he have a tumor?"

"No, he didn't have a tumor. But, according to the coroner, he was being poisoned. The coroner found arsenic in his system. It was only a matter of days before he would have died."

"Dear god," Rosemary uttered. "How could this have happened?"

"The coroner thinks he was getting small doses of poison every day for the past few months." He glanced at Tillie. "Didn't he complain about not feeling well while you were in Florida?"

"A few times, but then he started drinking a lot while we were gone. Perhaps, the alcohol covered the effects of the arsenic."

"That might be possible. It's something I need to check out." Austin pulled a pen out of his pocket and made a note on the paper. "Tillie, I need the names and addresses of the people you were staying with while you were in Florida."

"Of course," she replied.

"And, their phone number, if you have it," he added.

"I do." Tillie started to get up out of her chair, and, then, suddenly, she sat back in her chair and started to cry. "Mother, what is it? Are you okay?" Rosemary asked.

"No! I'm not okay," Tillie yelled. "I'm mad at myself for not seeing that something was seriously wrong with Lowell. I should have done something as soon as he started acting differently. It's my fault he's dead. I should have stayed with him the night we got home, but I was so mad at him for being drunk."

Rosemary handed her mother a tissue. "It's not your fault, Mother. How could you know?"

"Could you get those names and numbers for me, Tillie?" Chief Austin asked. "I'm sorry to rush you and I don't mean to be insensitive, but I need to get back to the station."

"Of course," Tillie said, wiping her eyes.

As soon as Tillie left the room, Austin leaned over to get closer to Joseph and Rosemary. "Here's the thing," he whispered. "What we have is a murder and an attempted murder. Tillie was around Lowell every day along with . . ." He hesitated. "Who are those people in Florida?"

"Lowell's cousin and his wife," Rosemary told him.

"So, it could be them who were trying to poison Lowell. The thing is, he was getting that arsenic from someone who was close to him."

"How does anyone get their hands on arsenic, anyway?" Rosemary asked.

"There are a lot of pesticides that have it in them. It's not that hard to come by," Austin replied. "And, then, on top of everything else, we have a possible break-in the day they get back home. I have a forensic team going through Lowell's house right now, trying to find any evidence that a break-in actually did occur."

"You can't seriously believe that Tillie would have tried to kill Lowell?" Joseph exclaimed.

"Right now, I have to have an open mind," Austin said. "I'm not ruling out anyone. And, remember, Tillie is the only heir to Lowell's estate and, as far as we know right now, the only one with a motive."

"That's true," Rosemary agreed. "But his cousin was his sole heir before he changed his will."

"Well, if that's the case, I would think he would have tried to poison Tillie and not Lowell."

A few hours later, Tillie was standing outside Lowell's home talking to Chief Austin. "I'm sorry, Dan, but I couldn't find one thing that's missing from the house. I forgot that Lowell transferred his coin collection to his safety deposit box before we left. At first, I thought it was missing. I guess I'm getting forgetful these days. However, if it was a robbery gone bad, the thief left without taking anything."

"It looks that way, but we can't find any evidence that his house was broken into. Of course, the girls did say that the house wasn't locked when they came over to drop off the scooter. Maybe, whoever it was, just walked right in," Chief Austin said.

"So, it could have been anyone. What happens now?" Tillie asked.

"I'm waiting for a call back from the Sheriff in Tampa. Until then, I'll just keep working with what I have now."

"It's for you, Chief," Sergeant Matt Haase yelled.

Chief Austin reached across his desk and picked up the phone. "Chief Austin," he said, waiting for the caller to identify himself. He straightened up in his chair, paying attention to the person on the other end. "Yes, Sir. That would be me. Thanks for calling back so fast."

He listened for a moment. "I've got the information right here. Ready?" Good. The name of Lowell Dobson's cousin is Charles Dobson. His wife's name is Marie." He listened to the caller for a moment. That's correct. He's Lowell Dobson's second cousin. I thought I'd fax you the autopsy report. I think it's enough for you to get a warrant and search their residence." He was silent, listening. "It had to be one of them or his lady friend that lives up here. Her name is Matilda Weiner, but everyone calls her Tillie," he told the caller. "I'll send Charles' and Marie's address along with the fax. Lowell and Tillie stayed with them from November to just a week ago, I believe. I can check those dates and get back to you."

Chief Austin was quiet for a few more moments, making notes as the Sheriff in Tampa talked to him. "That's right, Sheriff. Well, no. That's the strange thing. He didn't die from arsenic poison. He died from a blow to the head. But the doctor here said the arsenic would have killed him in a day or two." He listened, shaking his head in agreement with what the Sheriff was saying. "Only Mrs. Weiner, but I don't think she'd do it. They were planning on getting married in a couple of weeks."

Chief Austin sat back in his seat and switched

the phone to his other ear. "Ah huh. I understand. Well, let me know what you can do. I appreciate it. Bye." He looked over at Sergeant Haase. "Matt?"

"What?" Sergeant Haase asked as Austin hung up the phone.

"The sheriff will see what he can do. Fax all the information we have on Lowell's cousin and a copy of the autopsy report to him. Here's his fax number." Austin handed Haase a piece of paper.

"You don't really think that Tillie tried to poison Lowell, do you?" Haase asked Austin.

"Just between us? No. But, you just never know what a person is capable of. I'm constantly surprised by the actions of people."

"Yeah, but, Tillie? No way." Sergeant Haase said.

"I want a urine sample from her. Would you like to do the honors and go tell her? And, then drive her to the doctor?"

Sergeant Haase hesitated. "I guess I can," he replied after a few seconds. "But, why?"

"To see if she's ingested any arsenic, too. There's a good possibility that if Lowell's cousin did do this, he might have tried to poison Tillie, also. You know – kill two birds with one stone. Then, if they both died, he would be the sole beneficiary of Lowell's estate."

"Just how rich was Lowell, anyway?" Haase asked.

"Big rich. You'd never know it by the way he lived, but he was worth big bucks."

"What about Tillie?" Sergeant Haase inquired.

"Tillie has a few bucks, but nothing to speak of. The house is in her name, but she's leaving that to her daughter." Chief Austin thought for a moment. "You know, Matt, Tillie is over eighty. It doesn't make sense that she would try to kill Lowell for his money. I mean, how much longer would the two of them be around? She'd never be able to spend it all. More and more, I'm leaning toward the cousin. Let's just hope the Sheriff in Tampa finds something we can use."

"I sure hope so," Haase commented. "And, the fact that she had a big fight with Lowell and was calling off the wedding, is even more proof she probably didn't do it."

Chief Austin's head jerked up and he stared at Haase. "What do you mean, she was calling off the wedding?"

"You didn't know?"

"Hell, no, I didn't know."

"I heard she was so upset over his drinking that she wasn't going to marry him. So, why try to kill him if she wasn't going to marry him?"

"Well, that changes everything," Austin declared.

"What does it change?"

Austin didn't say anything.

"Chief?"

Chief Austin shook his head. "Just a moment." Finally, he looked over at Haase and shrugged. "Damned if I know, but it sure as hell must change something."

Sergeant Haase stood up and reached for his hat. "You know, Chief, Tillie is now a very rich woman. I sure hope the lab finds a little arsenic in her blood."

"Just make sure you stay with her while she pees."

"In the same room? She's not going to like that one little bit."

"No," Austin said, grinning. "Not in the same room. I mean stay near her, outside the bathroom door. Then, bag it and tag it, and get it back here so we can get it to forensics. You know, the chain of command and all that stuff. Although, you know, we might be too late. Arsenic usually doesn't show up in urine if it's over 48 hours. We should probably take a nail clipping or some hair, and send that out, too. That would give us a more accurate test."

"I'll make sure you get everything you need. Did she seem sick to you when you last talked to her?" Sergeant Haase asked.

"Not really, but she was pretty upset about Lowell."

"Yeah, and even if we find out who tried to poison Lowell, we still don't have a clue as to who actually did him in."

Seventeen

"So, what should she do now?" Rosemary asked Chief Austin.

"She should keep her appointments with the doctor, and make sure she takes the vitamin E and those other pills. Seriously, Rosemary, I wouldn't worry too much about it. Although she did have more arsenic in her system than normal, it wasn't as excessive as what we saw with Lowell."

Rosemary breathed out a sigh of relief. "I'm so glad to hear that. I was really worried about her."

"I know. How's she doing otherwise? You know, with losing Lowell and getting through the funeral and all. How's she handling everything?"

"Surprisingly well," Rosemary told him. "I guess by the time you reach her age, you get used to losing close friends and loved ones. She told me that you have to move on because you don't have enough life left to waste it mourning over the dead."

"I doubt they make 'em any tougher than Tillie," Austin said. "I'm just glad she's doing okay."

"She puts on a pretty good front. Sometimes I hear her crying at night, though."

"We all mourn in our own ways, I guess," Austin said.

"We do. But, knowing my mother, I suspect that you'll be getting a phone call from me one of these days telling you that she's gone missing again."

"She's back riding around on Red, then, is she?"

"She is. And, it seems she's found a few new friends with which she can go gallivanting all over the town. God help us all."

Chief Austin smiled. "Don't you worry. I'll tell my officers to keep an eye out for them and make sure they stay safe." Chief Austin pushed his chair away from the table and stood up. "Thanks for the coffee and sweet roll. It hit the spot."

"Are you going to let Lowell's attorney know that mother is no longer a suspect? He's been asking when he can start distributing funds."

"I'll give him a call. What in the world is Tillie going to do with all that money?"

Rosemary rolled her eyes. "God knows. Every day it's something else. I do think that she'll donate a lot of it. Lowell only had the one cousin down in Florida, and of course, seeing as how he tried to kill Lowell and Tillie, he'll probably be spending the rest of his life in jail."

"You know, Tillie was lucky that Charles Dobson didn't know that Lowell had changed his will until it was almost time for them to come home. There was no way he could have done much damage to Tillie with the short amount of time he had. Thank God, he wasn't smart enough to up her dosage and just gave her the same as he was giving Lowell." Chief Austin, who was leaning on the back of a chair, sat back down and reached for another sweet roll. "Okay?" he asked Rosemary, smiling.

"Of course. Help yourself. Would you like more coffee, too?"

"Thanks, but no. The roll is fine."

"Did you know that Charles used to live in Fall River when he was younger?" Rosemary asked him.

"After he graduated from college, he met and married Marie, who was raised in Beaver Dam. They lived there until he retired and, then, they moved to Florida. Marie's sister has a couple of boys and they still live in Beaver Dam. They came to Lowell's funeral, which was nice of them."

"Really? I never thought about checking out Marie's family. So, she would be the boys' aunt and Charles would be their uncle by marriage." Austin stuffed the rest of the sweet roll into his mouth and stood up. "I need to check out a few things, Rosemary," he said, chewing loudly.

Rosemary watched as he grabbed his hat, and headed out the front door. "Well, goodbye to you, too," she muttered.

"What was that all about?" Tillie asked as she walked into the kitchen.

"You're up. Did you have a good rest?"

"About as good as can be expected. When you have as many responsibilities as I have to deal with, it's hard to put your mind at ease."

"And, what would those be?" Rosemary asked, already knowing the answer.

"My estate, of course, and what to do with it. Of course, you know I'm leaving you my house. However, I wonder if you might want Lowell's house instead. It's a much newer home, it's bigger, and it's all on one floor. It would be better for you and Joseph as you get older. Of course, I could always put a stair chair lift in this house. Maybe, I'll do that anyway."

"Oh, Mother, I've lived here so long. I don't know if I would want to move."

130

"It's just a house, Rosemary."

"I know, but I was raised here and there are a lot of fond memories here."

"So, move and make some new memories. Anyway, I'm thinking about it, so find out how Joseph feels about it. I'm also thinking of moving to a retirement village. You know, one of those really fancy ones, where you get your meals and they do the housekeeping for you. I'd be around a lot of people my age and we could play cards and dance and have parties. What do you think about that?"

Rosemary's mouth dropped open. She stared at her mother, astounded by what she had just said. "But, I. . . I thought. . . I'm surprised. We talked about you moving into one of those places and you were dead set against it."

"Of course, I was. You were trying to get rid of me and put me in some crummy old home. Now, I can afford to live in a nice one. It's totally different from what you were going to do. But I haven't decided yet. I may just keep on living here."

Rosemary swallowed. "That would be nice, too."

"There are a lot of old people who live in those nice places that have scooters, too. Of course, they probably have real fancy ones."

"So, are you saying you're going to get a new scooter?" Rosemary asked.

Tillie stared at her. "Are you crazy? I would never get rid of Red. Honestly, Rosemary, sometimes I just don't understand your thinking."

Rosemary sighed. "Whatever you want, Mother."

Tillie chuckled.

"What's so funny?" Rosemary asked her.

"If I moved to one of those fancy places where everyone has a fancy scooter, we could call it 'Scooter Village'." She waited for Rosemary to say something. "Well?"

Rosemary smiled. "That's nice."

Tillie shook her head. "You never did have much of a sense of humor. However, I think I've found one thing I'm definitely going to do," Tillie said, grinning.

Rosemary looked at her, not saying anything.

"Well, don't you want to know?"

"Of course," Rosemary said, sighing. "What is it that you're going to do?"

"There are a lot of people, living right here in Columbus, who have trouble getting around. I bet a lot of them would love to have a scooter to ride. So, if they can't get one from Medicare, I'm going to be sure they get one from me. By the time I'm done, Rosemary, every old fart in this town will be running around on a brand-new scooter."

Joseph walked into the kitchen, said hi to Rosemary, opened the refrigerator door, and looked inside.

"Are you getting something or just cooling off?" Rosemary asked, sarcastically.

Joseph turned and looked at her. "Who bit you in the butt? I'm looking for a beer."

"I'm sorry I snapped at you. We're out of beer."

"Is Tillie bugging you again?"

"I swear, Joseph, she is driving me nuts with this money thing. She spends hours trying to figure

132

out how to spend it. Today, she decided to buy scooters for all the old people in town, wants us to move into Lowell's house, or she's gonna put a stairlift in this house, and she may just move into a fancy retirement village, whose name she is going to change to 'Scooter Village'. And, that was just this morning. God only knows what she's decided to do this afternoon."

Joseph grinned.

"I should have known you'd think this was funny. Well, you don't have to be home all day to listen to this crap."

"I'm sorry, Rosemary. I just don't know why you can't just roll with it. She's excited about the good she can do with the money. And, maybe moving into Lowell's old house isn't a bad idea. It is a ranch and it would be easier on all of us." He was quiet for a moment, thinking. "I like the idea. I've never been quite comfortable living here. You know, it is Tillie's house, not ours."

"Well, Lowell's house would be hers, too. You'd still be living in her house."

"Yeah, I know. But it would be different. Or, seeing as how you're going to inherit her house anyway, maybe she would give you Lowell's house now, with the understanding that she would continue to live with us," Joseph suggested.

"Either way, I'd still have her under my feet every day," Rosemary uttered.

Joseph stared at her. "I can't believe you just said that."

Rosemary turned away, her face turning red. "I

didn't mean that. I'm sorry. It's just that she wears me out sometimes."

"I know, but she means well."

"But I do like the idea of her moving into a nice retirement village. And, she can afford a nice one now. I think she'd be happy in one of them."

"No!" Joseph practically shouted. "Sorry, I didn't mean to raise my voice. Rosemary, do you know how much those places cost? It could virtually clean her out. We'd be left with nothing. No, I think Tillie should stay with us. It's for the best and if she wants to move to Lowell's house, then, that's what we'll do. Just be patient, okay? She doesn't have that much time left and she should be with family."

Stunned at her husband's comments, Rosemary stared at him. "It wouldn't clean her out, Joseph. It would barely put a dent in that money."

"Really? Just how much was old Lowell worth?"

Rosemary shook her head. "This isn't about the money." Rosemary stood up, grabbed her purse from the counter, and headed towards the door.

"Where are you going?" Joseph asked.

"For a ride. I've got to get out of here for a while and clear my head."

"What about dinner?"

"What about it?"

"Well, I'm hungry. When will you be back?" Joseph asked, completely confused by the way she was acting.

"I'll be back when I'm back," Rosemary told him. "For god's sake, Joseph, you're not a baby. Make yourself something to eat if you're hungry." She opened the door and started walking out of the house.

"Rosemary," Joseph called after her."

Rosemary turned and looked at him. "What?"

"Will you pick up a six-pack of beer on your way home?"

RED . . . . Susan L Pare'

July, 2018

RED . . . . Susan L Pare'

Eighteen

"Well, that's the last of it," Lynn stated, as she looked around the living room. "It looks so different without all the furniture in it."

"Smaller. Right?" Stacy asked.

"Yeah, I guess."

"When do the new owners take possession?" Stacy inquired, as she bent down and picked up a piece of cardboard that had been left on the floor.

"Next week. Mom wanted to have enough time between closings to be sure everything was emptied out and she had time to come in and clean."

Stacy grinned. "Clean what? You could eat off the floor, this place is so spotless."

"She does keep a clean house, doesn't she?" Lynn declared.

"Well, shall we lock up and get out of here?" Stacy asked.

"Nope," Lynn said. "We've got one last thing to do." Smiling, she reached into her oversized purse and pulled out two plastic cups and two miniature-sized bottles of Jack Daniels."

Stacy grinned when she saw the liquor. "Make, it one for my baby, and one more for the road," she sang. "How many of those bottles have you got?"

Lynn laughed. "Probably, not enough. Let's see if there's any ice left in the fridge."

"I doubt it," Stacy uttered. "I'm sure Mom moved that, too."

"Funny," Lynn said.

"I know."

"There's ice," Lynn exclaimed, as she opened the freezer door. She reached in and pulled out a few cubes and dropped them into the cups. She handed the miniature bottles to Stacy. "Open them, will you?"

Lynn held the cups, while Stacy emptied a bottle of the liquor into each one of the paper containers. Lynn handed her sister one of the cups and smiled sadly.

"Well, here's to the end of a long episode, so . . ." Stacy started singing.

"Isn't it a brief episode?" Lynn asked her.

"Not in this case, it isn't. It's been a long one," Stacy replied.

"So, make it one for my baby, and one more for the road," the sisters sang.

"Bottoms up," Lynn toasted, tears running down her cheeks.

"Back atcha, sis," Stacy said. "Down the hatch."

"Through the lips and over the gums, look out stomach here she comes," Lynn said, smiling through her tears.

"Here's to those who wish us well; and, those that don't can go to hell."

Lynn laughed. "We can do this all day, you know, or actually drink this shit," she said.

"You're right. No sense in stalling any longer. And, this is not shit." She bit her bottom lip, trying to hold back the tears. "You know, this is probably the last time we'll be in this house. So, here's to ya, Sis." Stacy took a drink of Jack Daniels and swallowed. "Smooth," she said trying not to cry, as she watched Lynn lift her cup and drink.

"Well, you girls took your sweet time getting over here," Rosemary said, as her two daughters walked into the house. "What took you so long?"

"Just saying goodbye to the old house," Stacy said, looking at Lynn and grinning.

"I guess I'll be going," Lynn told her mom. "I've got plans and I need to get home and clean up."

"Bailing on us, huh, Sis?" Junior said as he walked by her, carrying a large box.

"Junior?" Rosemary called to him. "Where are you taking that box?"

"To the living room."

"No. It's for the kitchen. Just set it down here on the counter, please." She looked at Lynn and Stacy. "I can't believe how much stuff we have. It never ends."

"That's what happens when you live in the same house forever. You never weed out the junk."

"Well, it's not just that, you know. We had to decide what to get rid of and what stuff of Lowell's we'd keep. We tried to pick the best and sold off the rest."

"And, a great job you did, Mom," Lynn said. "Where's Grams? I want to say goodbye."

"I have no idea," Rosemary said. "She's off somewhere visiting friends. It's just as well. I get more accomplished when she's not here telling me what goes where. I'll finish her room up first, so she'll be comfortable when she gets back."

"I'll be here for a little while yet," Stacy said. "Why don't I do that?"

Rosemary smiled. "Why, thank you, Stacy. That would be wonderful. Do you know which room is hers?"

"No. Do you want to show me?"

"It's the master bedroom," Rosemary said, quietly. "It's the one off of the living room. You know, the big one, with a private bathroom. And, French doors. I guess she wanted to be in the same room where she slept with Lowell. I never approved of that, you know. Those two sleeping together at their age. I'll never know what . . ." Rosemary looked away, realizing that she was getting louder by the second. "Your father and I have a smaller bedroom in the back, off the hallway," she continued, once again speaking softly. "But, it's a nice room, so we'll do just fine."

"You'll have to show us that room, too," Stacy said.

"Why?" Rosemary asked. "It's just a plain old bedroom."

Stacy glanced over a Lynn. "Lynn, would you like to help me for a minute?"

Lynn hesitated. "Well, I really should go. . . Of course," she said when she saw the pleading look on her sister's face.

As soon as they were in Tillie's new bedroom, Stacy grabbed Lynn's arm. "Please, don't leave me alone with Mom. She's about to blow."

"Just stay out of her way. Finish getting Grams' room put together and get out of here."

"Please, I'm begging you. Stay with me."

Lynn laughed. "Stop being so dramatic. You can handle it."

"Not like you. You're better at it than I am."

Lynn looked at her watch. "All right. I can give

142

you half an hour and that's it."

Stacy glanced around the bedroom and at all the unpacked boxes sitting on the floor. "Well, then, let's get our asses moving, 'cause we got a lot to do and not a whole lot of time to do it in."

Forty-five minutes later, Lynn kissed her sister and mother goodbye. Rosemary stood in the doorway of Tillie's bedroom and smiled. "You girls did a wonderful job. Thank you, Stacy."

"You're welcome, Mom. I need to leave, but I'll be back in an hour or so. I'm pretty sure Simon is coming back with me, so Dad will have some help moving the heavier furniture."

"Junior is still here," Rosemary said. "He can help. You don't have to come back. You've done enough."

"And, I can do more. If Simon helps, it will get done sooner. Plus, you guys don't have anything here for dinner, and I'm going to bring back some food. I know you hate fast food, but I'll get Culvers or something."

"Thank you. That would be a big help if you want to do that."

"How about Culver's chicken sandwiches? I think everyone likes those. And, some fries, of course. Do you have anything here to drink?"

"Stacy, anything you get will be fine." Rosemary looked over at her daughter, a confused look on her face.

"What?" Stacy asked.

"Are you eating meat again? I thought you were

143

a vegetarian."

"Mom, I'll get a salad or something. I'm only a vegetarian in front of Simon and his health-nut friends. The rest of the time, I eat meat."

"Isn't that being deceitful?" Rosemary inquired.

"It's easier than having to fight with him about it."

"Well, I don't believe in lying to your husband, Stacy. It just isn't right."

"Right or wrong, that's the way it is and I'd appreciate it if you didn't say anything."

"Well, if it comes up, I'm certainly not going to lie for you."

Stacy frowned. "And, just why would it come up?"

Rosemary shrugged. "You just never know."

"I don't know why you even had to bring it up now." Stacy grabbed her purse off the counter and headed for the back door. "I'll see you later," she told her mother.

"How long will you be?" Rosemary called out, as the door slammed shut.

Nineteen

"I can't believe that you're already settled in," Lynn exclaimed. "It's only been a week and there's not one box left to be unpacked."

"Your dad was a big help," Rosemary commented. "He still has the garage to straighten up, but, basically, we're done."

"You've even hung the pictures. Wow, Mom. You're something else."

"I'm going to give Minnie Williams Blue," Tillie interjected.

Lynn glanced over at her. "You're doing what?"

"You remember my friend Minnie Williams. Well, she doesn't have a scooter, so I'm giving her Blue. Joseph wants it out of the garage and she doesn't have one, so I'm giving it to her."

"I thought she was ill," Rosemary said.

"She was. And, now she feels better. I told her she had to keep the name, though."

"That's nice of you, Mother," Rosemary declared. "Anyway, I didn't hang all of them," she told Lynn, getting back to their original conversation. "I thought you kids might like some of them, and I have way too many."

"Which pictures are you talking about?" Lynn asked.

"Most of them are old family pictures of your grandparents and great-grandparents. You kids should have them."

"Are you sure you want to get rid of them, Mom?"

"I'm sure."

"What about Dad?"

"He could care less. I put them in one of the spare bedrooms. Why don't you take a look before you leave and decide which ones you want?" Rosemary asked Lynn.

"I'm starting a scooter club," Tillie declared.

Rosemary rolled her eyes and sighed. "Maybe, you'd like to take a look now," she suggested to her daughter.

Lynn, who was grinning, looked at her grandmother. "You're doing what?"

"I'm starting a club for us old farts with scooters. We're going to meet once a week. . ." She hesitated. "Maybe, once a month would be better." She thought for a moment. "Anyway, we're going to meet for lunches and go for rides around town and go to the park and go swimming."

Lynn laughed. "You're going swimming at the park?"

"Why not? We need the exercise and swimming is good for you."

"What else are you planning to do?" Lynn said, grinning.

"For god's sake, Lynn, stop encouraging her," Rosemary said.

"I'm not. I'm interested, that's all," Lynn told her mother.

Tillie smiled. "Well, I'm glad somebody is interested. Your mother could care less about what I do."

"Well, I think a scooter club is a great idea,"

Lynn said. "It gives you something to do and gets you out of the house," she said, emphasizing 'out of the house', while she looked at her mother.

"All right. I get it," Rosemary said. "Enough, now, about those damn scooters."

"Where do you plan on holding these meetings?" Lynn asked Tillie.

Rosemary stared at her daughter. "Why do you hate me?" she asked, after a few seconds.

"Well, here, of course," Tillie told Lynn.

"Here?" Rosemary said loudly. "Why here?"

"Why not? We've got enough room and it is my house."

Rosemary pushed her chair away from the kitchen table and stood up. She looked at Lynn and shook her head.

"Where are you going?" Lynn asked.

"I need to go lie down," Rosemary told her, as she walked out of the room.

Tillie picked up her cup and finished the last of her coffee. She put the cup back on the saucer and looked at Lynn, a questioning look on her face.

"What?" Lynn asked.

"Is it just me or does your mother seem a little touchy lately?"

Joseph looked over at the old grandfather's clock and smiled. It was exactly one o'clock and his family was seated at the dining room table. "It's nice to know that we're running on time today. Your mother has outdone herself today."

Rosemary put the platter in front of Joseph and

147

handed him the carving knife. "Everything looks wonderful," he said, as he started carving the huge roast. He looked up at Rosemary, who was still standing alongside him. "What is it?" he asked.

"Mom, are you okay," Stacy asked, as she noticed her mother starting to cry.

"I'm fine. It's just that this . . ." She wiped her eyes with her apron. "This is the first time that the entire family has been together in a long time. Simon, I'm so glad you could make it today."

"I'm glad to be here," Simon told her. "I know I miss most of these Sunday get-togethers, but it's important that I coach these kids. A lot of them come from one-parent homes. The extra attention I can give them seems to be important."

"Of course, it is," Rosemary agreed. "And, David and Lisa. You're getting so big."

"Mother, you just saw them a couple of days ago. What is going on with you, anyway?" Stacy asked.

"Yeah, Mom, what's up? You're acting kind of weird," Junior said, as he reached for the bowl of potatoes.

Rosemary walked around the table and sat down across from Joseph. "I'm sorry if appreciating my family is acting weird. Shall we bow our heads and pray?"

"In the name of the Father, Son, and Holy Ghost," everyone mumbled, as they crossed themselves. "Bless us, Oh Lord, and these Thy gifts, which we are about to receive from Thy bounty, through Christ our Lord. Amen."

"So, Lynn, what's going on with you?" Junior

asked, as soon as the prayer was over.

Lynn looked up at him, surprised at his interest in her life. "Since when do you care what . . ." She hesitated, as she realized what he was doing and smiled at her brother. "Well, since you asked, I had quite a surprise the other day."

"What was that?" Stacy inquired, joining in the conversation.

"Do you remember a cop by the name of Matt Haase?"

Joseph looked up from his plate and stared at his daughter. "What did you do?"

Lynn laughed. "Nothing, Dad. I didn't do anything. Why would you ask that?"

"Because it's you, that's why."

"Well, I didn't do anything wrong, so don't worry."

"I know him," Joseph told her. "He's a nice guy."

"Well, what did he want?" Stacy asked her sister.

"He asked me out on a date," Lynn said, grinning.

"What?" Stacy exclaimed. "I didn't know you knew him."

"I hardly do. It took me by surprise."

"Are you going to go, Aunt Lynn?" Lisa asked.

"I'm not sure. I told him I'd let him know, but I'm not sure I want to date a cop from Columbus. Or, a cop from any town, as far as that goes."

"You could do worse, Lynn," Joseph said. "You should at least go out with him. What do you have to lose?"

"I guess," Lynn agreed.

"You're not getting any younger, you know," Rosemary commented. "It's about time you found a nice young man and settled down. And, we could use a few more grandchildren. Right, Joseph?"

Lynn looked at Stacy and shrugged. "What's your opinion, Sis? Should I give it a try?"

"Well, you know, those few good eggs you've got left aren't going to last forever," Stacy said, imitating an old lady with a crackling voice.

Lisa looked at her mother, confused by her comment. "What eggs?" she asked.

Tillie looked up from her plate, suddenly paying attention to the conversation. "Rosemary, that reminds me. Would you mind making some deviled eggs for my next scooter meeting? Yours are so delicious and I can never make them as good as you do."

As soon as lunch was over, Joseph headed for the couch and turned on the television. Within minutes, he was snoring.

"Dad?" Lynn whispered, not wanting her mother to hear her.

Joseph stirred and rolled over onto his side.

Lynn reached down and lightly shook her father. "Dad, wake up. We need to talk."

As Joseph opened his eyes, he passed wind. He sighed deeply and looked up at Lynn. "What? What is it?"

Lynn stepped back from her father, waving her hand back and forth in front of her face. "Geez, Dad. Oh, my god, that stinks."

Junior, who had just walked into the room,

150

laughed. "Now I know how to get rid of you," he joked.

"I think you're right. I think Dad's trying to kill me," Lynn replied. She watched as her dad sat up.

"What is it?" he asked. He sniffed the air. "Was that me?" he asked Lynn.

"We need to talk," Lynn told him.

"Can't it wait?" Joseph asked.

"No. And, we need to do it before Mom finishes up in the kitchen."

Joseph yawned. He looked at his two children and sighed. "Now what?"

"You need to take Mom on a vacation. Anywhere you want to go, but she needs to get out of here for a while and get some rest," Junior told his father. "I don't know if you're aware of it, Dad, but she's about ready to have a breakdown. She gets upset over just about anything and she's . . ." Junior hesitated. He looked at Lynn.

"She's angry all the time, Dad," Lynn continued. "Selling the old house and moving in here and dealing with Grams has just been too much for her. We're really worried about her and we think it would be a good idea if you two took a trip. You know, get her out of here for a while and away from Grams."

Joseph stared at his children. "What the hell are you talking about? There's nothing wrong with your mother. She's fine."

"No, Dad, she isn't. Think about it. Just the way she acted at lunch today, getting all teary-eyed and emotional. That's not Mom," Junior said.

Joseph pursed his lips and took a deep breath. He slowly let it out and shook his head up and down.

"You may be right. She has changed since Tillie came back from Florida. She was really happy while your grandmother was gone."

"Everything might have been okay if Lowell hadn't died and Tillie had married him. But there have been so many changes in the past few months and we think mom is just worn out," Lynn added. "What do you say, Dad? Can you get away for a few weeks?"

"Maybe, I could make it a surprise," Joseph replied.

"No!" Lynn and Junior both exclaimed at the same time.

"Why not?" Joseph asked.

"Mom hates surprises. You know that. No, it would be better if you told her. That way, she can get excited about going on a vacation, decide what clothes to take, maybe go shopping, and take care of everything. She's best when she's got a project to do and this might help before you ever leave," Lynn told him.

Joseph thought for a moment. "All right, but what about Tillie?"

"Stacy and I will take turns staying with her during the week and Lynn will do weekends," Junior said. "Don't worry about her. We've got it covered."

Joseph sat back on the couch and smiled. "Well, then, I guess all that's left is to decide where I take your mother. Now, if you don't mind, I'd like to finish my nap."

"Thanks, Dad," Lynn said.

"And, I think I feel another fart coming, so you might want to clear the room."

"Gross," Lynn yelled, as she ran out of the room, bumping into Stacy.

"What's the matter?" Stacy asked.

"Brown thunder warning," Lynn declared. "Stay clear of Dad."

Twenty

"Oh, dear god," Rosemary exclaimed. "How many were hurt? What about my mother?" She let out a sigh of relief and sat down on a kitchen chair. "Well, thank goodness for that. She's where? Well, if she wasn't hurt, why is she at the hospital?"

Rosemary listened to the person on the other end of the phone, shaking her head in agreement. "I'll be there in a few minutes and thank you so much for calling." Shaking as she hung up the phone, Rosemary didn't move for a few moments, trying to get her wits together. Finally, she picked up her phone, hit Stacy's speed dial number, and waited.

"Stacy, thank god I caught you. I was afraid you'd be out somewhere."

"It's a cell phone, Mom. It doesn't make any difference where I am when you call."

"That's right. I'm so upset; I guess I'm not thinking straight."

Stacy felt her heart speed up, concerned over what her mother was about to tell her. "Why are you upset?"

"It's grandma. She's at the hospital and I was wondering if . . ."

"What happened?" Stacy interrupted. "Is she okay?"

"She's fine," Rosemary told her. "But, some of her friends got hurt and she went with them to the hospital."

"Well, that's good news, isn't it? I mean that grandma is okay, not that her friends are hurt."

"I know what you meant," Rosemary replied. "Can you go pick her up from the hospital and bring her home?"

"Well, I guess. Why can't you go get her?"

"Because, Stacy, to be very honest with you, I'm afraid I'll wring her wrinkled old neck. I knew something like this would happen. Her and those old people riding all over town on those damn scooters. I knew someone would get hurt someday."

"What happened?" Stacy asked.

"From what I understand, your grandmother and four or five of her delinquent friends were driving their scooters around town. They were on James Street, going east down that damn hill. Well, one of the ladies – I don't know which one. Anyway, one of her scooter's wheels went down that little step they added to that slanted sidewalk and tipped over. I guess it was like a chain reaction, with one scooter after another driving into each other. Anyway, a couple of her friends hit the cement hard and got hurt. They have a lot of scrapes and bruises and a broken bone or two. Fortunately, your grandmother was in front of everyone, leading the way, just like she always does, and she's okay."

Stacy closed her eyes, picturing the scene.

"Are you still there?" Rosemary shouted into the phone.

"Yes, Mother, I'm still here."

"Well, will you go pick her up or not?"

"Of course, I'll go get her. I need to pick Lisa up from the park, anyway. Grandma can go with me."

"Her scooter is at the hospital. They want it

picked up, also," Rosemary told her.

"Who is they?"

"He. He wants it picked up. I don't remember his name. It's the person who called from the hospital."

"Why is her scooter at the hospital? Was it injured, too?"

"This isn't funny, Stacy."

"I know. Sorry, Mother."

"Your grandmother insisted they take it with them. She said she wouldn't go and get checked out if they didn't take it along with her.

"Well, if she wasn't hurt, why did they need to check her out?

Rosemary sighed. "I don't know, Stacy. Will you just go get her, please?"

"No problem. I'll get Grandma and her scooter. I'll call you later," Stacy told her, wanting to get off the phone.

"Thank you," Rosemary said.

"You know, I think I'll bring grandma home with me for dinner. Simon is grilling salmon tonight. She might enjoy that." Stacy added.

"I've already started dinner. You don't need to feed her, too. Just pick her up, please."

"I think it would be nice if you and Dad had some time alone tonight. Don't worry. I'll bring Grandma home safe and sound. Bye." Stacy hung up her phone and grinned. Lynn is never going to believe this one, she thought, as she grabbed her car keys and headed out the door.

"Are you sure you're okay, Tillie?" Joseph asked.

"I'm fine. It was the people behind me that got hurt. Poor Minnie is going to be in the hospital for quite a while."

"What happened to her?" Joseph inquired, wondering why Rosemary was giving him a dirty look.

"She has a broken arm and wrist. Her leg is all banged up. She got the worst of it. Everyone else is going to be okay. They all went home."

"Well, you shouldn't have given her Lowell's old scooter. I knew something like this would happen," Rosemary snapped.

"Maybe not," Tillie replied. "But she was having a good time and I'm not sorry I gave it to her." She stood up and looked at Joseph. "I'm tired. I'm going to bed. Good night."

"Good night, Tillie. I'm glad you're okay."

Rosemary hesitated a moment. "Me, too. I'm glad you didn't get hurt. Good night, Mother.

As Tillie opened the door to her bedroom, she turned and looked at Rosemary and her son-in-law. "When are you leaving on your trip?"

"We leave Saturday," Rosemary told her.

"That's only a few days away," Tillie said. "Are you excited?"

"I am," Joseph replied. "It's been a long time since just the two of us have been on a vacation. I'm looking forward to it."

"That's nice. Well, good night, again," Tillie said, as she went into her bedroom and shut the door.

"It's time to turn down the TV," Rosemary told Joseph.

"I did already. She can't hear it in there."

"We should have had that room, not her. If she was in a back bedroom, we wouldn't have to tiptoe around every night when she goes to bed."

"It's fine, Rosemary. I don't mind," Joseph commented.

"Well, I do," Rosemary told him.

"Can you turn that TV down?" Tillie yelled from her bedroom. "I'm trying to sleep in here."

Rosemary sighed. "See what I mean? I swear, someday I'm going to smother that woman."

Twenty-one

"Good morning, Dan," Rosemary said, as she opened the door. "Come on in."

Chief Austin glanced around the house and smiled. "Man, this place looks like you've lived here for years. I can't believe you've settled in already. That was fast."

Rosemary smiled. "We were settled a week after we moved. I don't like clutter and Joseph and the kids were a big help." She motioned to a chair by the kitchen table. "Coffee?"

"Don't mind if I do," Austin replied, as he sat down.

"I've heard your dad isn't doing too well," Rosemary commented.

Austin smiled. "He had a little thing with his heart a few weeks ago, but he's doing okay now. I figure he'll be around for quite a while. Grandpa lived into his nineties, you know."

"Augie was such a nice man. I bet he was proud that Tommy and you both followed in his footsteps," Rosemary said. "Anyway, what brings you here this morning?" Rosemary asked him, as she poured coffee into a mug and handed it to him.

"I thought I'd give you an update regarding Lowell's murder."

"I was wondering about that," Rosemary said. "It's been a while."

"I know and I think we've exhausted every lead we had. I thought Marie Dobson's nephews might have had something to do with it, but they both have

159

airtight alibis."

"Well, it made sense that it might be them. If she knew that her husband was trying to kill Lowell, she might have asked her nephews to do him in after that didn't work."

"That's what I thought," Austin said. "I figured they were planning to kill both Lowell and Tillie, but Tillie didn't stay with Lowell that night. Regardless, both men are in the clear."

"Do you think you'll ever find out who did it?" Rosemary asked.

"You never know. Just when you think it's gonna be a cold case forever, something pops up and you solve it. At least we got Charles Dobbs for attempted murder. That's better than nothing."

"I guess. But, when Lowell died, it affected a lot of lives. It would be nice for my mom to have closure."

"How's she doing, anyway? I heard there was a little pile-up downtown the other day," Austin said, grinning.

Rosemary gave him a look. "It's not funny, Dan."

"Sorry, I didn't mean to make light of it."

"Mom is fine, but a few of her friends got hurt. I knew something like this would happen one day."

"Hell, the whole town knew it. The way that sidewalk was repaired is a joke."

Rosemary looked surprised. "You're blaming the sidewalk?"

"Of course. It's a real hazard."

"It's not the sidewalk that's the hazard. It's Tillie and her scooter club. That's your real problem."

"I don't know I'd say that, Rosemary. They're

just a bunch of old people trying to enjoy what little life they have left. It was an accident and it could have happened to anyone."

Rosemary shook her head. "So, she's got you fooled, too."

Chief Austin finished the last of his coffee, stood up, and put his cup in the sink. "Anyway, I just wanted to fill you in on the case. I heard you and Joe are taking a little trip."

Rosemary smiled. "We are. It's our first vacation in a long time with just the two of us."

"Well, good for you. I hope you have a wonderful time." He hesitated a moment. "I probably shouldn't ask, but do you have someone to stay with Tillie? I could check in on her if you want."

"Thanks, but the family has it covered. I'm going to go and have a good time and not think about this place until we get back. It's been a rough few months and I can't wait to get away and relax."

"When are you leaving?"

"Tomorrow and it isn't soon enough."

"It sounds like you really do need to get away." He picked up his hat and walked to the door. "Send me a postcard," he called out, as he left the house.

"I'll be there around eight tomorrow morning," Lynn told her mother. "Is that soon enough?"

"That's a little early. We aren't leaving for the airport until around eleven, but come when you want."

"Well, then, maybe I'll sleep an extra hour. I guess I'll be there around ten."

"I appreciate you doing this, Lynn. I know you're

giving up two weekends to help out."

"Seriously, Mom? I love being around Grams. This is a treat for me."

"Try to keep her busy and off that damn scooter. Okay?"

"Mom, you're already worrying about nothing. I'll take good care of her."

"I know you will," Rosemary said.

"I've got to run. I'll see you in the morning."

"So, is everything set?" Joseph asked.

Rosemary jumped at the sound of his voice. She put her hand over her heart and cried out, "My god, you almost gave me a heart attack."

Joseph smiled. "Sorry, I didn't mean to scare you."

"I didn't hear you come in. How long have you been home?"

"Not that long. I was doing some work in the yard."

"Did you get the rose bushes planted?"

"I did. And, I asked the Sullivan boy to water them while we're gone."

"That's good, dear. By the way, Chief Austin came by this morning," Rosemary told him.

"And?"

"Nothing. He said they haven't got a clue who might have killed Lowell."

"What about those nephews?" Joseph asked.

"Nope. They have alibis."

Joseph sighed. "Well, hopefully, something will turn up. Now, how about we forget all about Tillie and

162

get packed?"

Rosemary closed her eyes and sighed. "That's easier said than done, you know."

"Try."

"What do you want for dinner tonight?" Rosemary asked him.

"Oh, no. You're not cooking tonight. Why don't we go to the Capri? I'm in the mood for a good steak."

"I don't know if I want to go out and eat. I don't feel very hungry."

"Maybe not right now, but you will be in a couple of hours."

Twenty-two

Chief Daniel Austin grumbled as he reached for the phone that was on his nightstand. He glanced at the clock and swore. It was a little after one a.m. and a call at this time of the night was never good news. He picked up the phone and whispered, "Austin here."

"It's Lee, Dan."

"Hold on." Trying not to wake his wife, Austin exited the bed and walked into the living room. "What's up, Lee?"

"Sorry to wake you, Chief. It's Tillie Weiner. She's been missing since yesterday afternoon. Her daughter just called, all upset, and asked for some help. I'm heading over there now."

"Iser scoomissing?" Austin asked while trying to stifle a yawn.

"What did you say?"

"Is her scooter missing?" Austin repeated.

"Yeah, the scooter is gone, too. At least, they can't find it and, according to Rosemary Larson, they've looked everywhere."

Austin sighed. "I'll meet you there in a few minutes."

"I can handle it," Wong said. "I just wanted to fill you in. I probably wouldn't have bothered you if it was anyone else, but with everything that has happened . . . You know, with Lowell and all."

"You did the right thing. I'll see you in a few." Austin ended the call, walked back into his bedroom, and reached for his pants.

"Tillie again?" his wife asked. "I heard you say

scooter."

"She's missing."

"At this time of night?"

"Yeah, and I don't like it one bit."

"How long, Rosemary?" Austin asked again.

"I really don't know. Joseph said he didn't see her or her scooter when he came home from work."

"And, that would be about five-thirty or six?" Austin asked.

"No, it was earlier than that. He left work early yesterday. He had some last-minute packing to do." Rosemary turned towards her husband. "Joseph, what time did you get home yesterday?"

Joseph shrugged. "I'm not exactly sure. I left work around one-thirty or so. I spent a little time pulling a few weeds in the flower beds before I came inside. I guess I noticed that Red wasn't on the front porch around two-thirty or so. That's about right. I remember wondering where Tillie was off to now."

"I thought she was in her bedroom taking a nap," Rosemary added. "When I went to check on her, she wasn't there."

"So, you don't have any idea what time she left the house or where she was going?" Austin inquired.

"None. When she wasn't home by dark, we thought she might have been at one of her friend's houses. So, before we called the police, Joseph drove around trying to spot her scooter."

"No luck there," Joseph told Austin. "I didn't want to wake people up and ask them if they knew where she was, but maybe I should have."

"I'll have one of my officers do that." Austin looked over at Rosemary. "Could you write out a list of her friends for me? Their addresses would be good, too, if you know them."

"I'm pretty sure Mother has them all in her address book. Give me a minute," Rosemary said, as she stood up and walked to Tillie's bedroom.

Chief Austin glanced around the living room. "This is a nice house," he commented.

"It is," Joseph agreed. "Whoever built this place didn't spare any expense. I've never seen a house that was so well insulated. Our heating bills should be pretty low this winter."

"Do you have any idea what's going on with Tillie, Joseph?" Austin asked.

Joseph shook his head no. "I haven't a clue. All I know is if she isn't back home by eleven o'clock, Rosemary and I won't be going on our vacation."

"You don't think she is hiding away someplace just to ruin your trip, do you?" Austin asked.

Joseph looked at him, surprised by the question. "No way. Tillie wouldn't do that. I mean, she may not always get along with Rosemary, but she isn't mean. No. I can't believe she'd do that."

"Do what?" Rosemary asked as she walked into the room.

"Daniel thought maybe she was hiding somewhere just to ruin our vacation," Joseph told her.

"Really?" Rosemary said. "I never thought of that, but I wouldn't put it past her."

"Rosemary! How can you say that?" Joseph exclaimed. "Tillie would never do something so mean."

"Well, I'm not sure if she would or not. But it wouldn't surprise me if she shows up about the same time our plane is taking off."

"I'm going to take a look around outside and, then, head over to the station. I need to call everyone in and set up a search party." Austin looked at his watch. "It's almost three-thirty and I'd like to begin the search as soon as it gets light outside. In the meanwhile, I'll contact her friends and find out if anyone knows anything."

"I'd like to help," Joseph told him.

"I'll let you know if I need you," Austin said. "Right now, it's best if you and Rosemary stay here just in case Tillie shows up."

"You'll call us right away if you hear anything, won't you?" Rosemary asked Chief Austin.

"You'll be the first ones I call. But, right now, say a little prayer that we find her safe and sound."

Sergeant Matt Haase looked up as the kitchen door opened. He smiled when he saw Lynn walk in. "Hi," he greeted her.

Lynn smiled back. "Hi. Is there any news about Grams?"

"We've got everyone out looking, but no luck so far. Do you have any idea where she could be?"

"None. But I do know that this is serious, Matt. Grams would never stay away this long unless something was wrong. She would have called if she needed help."

"Her cell phone is off. We can't get a location."

"Oh, Lynn, thank god you're here," Rosemary

said as she walked into the kitchen. "Do you want some breakfast?"

Lynn walked over to her mother and hugged her. "How about I fix you some breakfast? You look terrible, Mother. Have you had any rest at all?"

"How could I sleep with your grandmother missing?"

"Are Stacy and Junior here?" Lynn asked.

"Junior's out looking for your grandmother and Stacy will be over later." Rosemary glanced over at the counter. "The coffee is almost gone. I need to make . . ."

"What you need is to go sit down. I'll make the coffee," Lynn interrupted. "Where's dad?"

"He's somewhere outside. He said he needed to go for a walk." Suddenly, Rosemary started to cry.

"Come on, Mom." Lynn took Rosemary by the arm and walked her to the couch in the living room. "Why don't you just lie back for a while and get some rest?" Lynn waited until her mother was on the couch, then, took a small throw and covered her up. "It's going to be okay. I'll go make that coffee now."

"What if something horrible has happened?" Rosemary said softly. "I've been so horrible to her. I'll never forgive myself."

"This isn't your fault," Lynn told her. "You know Grams is always doing something silly. She probably got stuck in a rut on Red someplace and wouldn't leave him. Or, maybe the battery died. They'll probably find her sitting on that darn scooter waiting for someone to come rescue her."

"Do you think so?" Rosemary asked.

"Of course, I do," Lynn replied. She walked back into the kitchen and looked at Sergeant Haase. "Why are you here, anyway?"

"It's common for someone to stay with the family while this type of search is going on. I volunteered," he said smiling.

"Well, I'm glad you did." As Lynn took the coffee pot and started to rinse it out, she noticed her hands were shaking. "My god, I'm a nervous wreck," she told Haase.

"Why don't you let me do that?" he said and walked over to the sink.

"I'm fine," Lynn said, jumping as his phone rang, startling her. She dropped the glass pot into the sink, shattering it. "Shit," she cried out.

"Where?" Sergeant Haase asked the person who called. "I see. Was there any sign of . . ." He glanced over at Lynn. "Hold on a minute," he told the caller. "You're fading out. I need to go outside."

Lynn watched him as he walked out of the kitchen and stood in the driveway, completing his phone call.

Twenty-three

Sergeant Haase put his phone in his pocket and walked to the back of the house. Although it was some distance away, with trees and bushes blocking most of the view, the Crawfish River was visible from where Haase was standing. He sighed deeply, not looking forward to talking to the Larson family.

"It was bad news, wasn't it?" Lynn said softly. "That phone call you just had."

Haase turned around, surprised he hadn't heard her coming up behind him. "It could be. We don't know for sure yet."

"Tell me."

"I should go inside and talk to your parents first."

Lynn stared at him. "Tell me."

"It may be nothing. They found her scooter."

"And, Grams?" Lynn asked. "Did they find her, too?"

"No. And, that's the good news."

"Where did they find Red?"

"In the river."

Lynn looked stunned. "In the river? Gram's scooter was in the river? Oh, my god, Matt."

"Don't jump to conclusions, Lynn," he told her. "Until we find your grandmother, she's alive. Got it?"

"But, in the river? Oh, dear god." Trying to hold it together, Lynn closed her eyes and took a deep breath. "Exactly where was it?"

"The search party found it a few houses up from Tillie's old house. Just up from the last house on the street."

"You can't tell Mom and Dad."

"I have to," Haase said. "They have a right to know."

"No," Lynn said. "They're upset enough already, especially Mom. If she hears about this, it will put her over the edge. Wait a little longer. Please," Lynn pleaded.

"I don't know . . ."

"Please, Matt. Give it an hour or so. Please."

Sergeant Haase shook his head. "I shouldn't wait. I promised I'd keep them informed." He looked at Lynn, watching as she brushed the tears away with the back of her hand. "One hour. That's all I can do."

An hour later, Sergeant Haase waited while Joseph and Rosemary sat down on the couch.

"Wait for me," Lynn called out. "I'm getting a coffee. Does anyone want anything?"

"No, thank you," her mom replied.

"How about you, Dad? Matt?"

"I'm fine," Sergeant Haase told her.

"Me, too," Joseph said. He glanced over at Lynn. "How did you make coffee? You broke the pot."

"It's instant. I hate it but it's better than nothing."

"Did you hear something about Mom?" Rosemary asked him.

"I have some news for you. But, please, don't jump to any conclusions over what I'm about to tell you. Okay?"

Rosemary reached over and took her husband's

hand and held it. "Go on," she said.

"Tillie's scooter was found about an hour ago. We thought it was . . ."

"What the hell do you mean an hour ago?" Joseph yelled. "Why weren't we told . . ."

"Hold on," Haase interrupted. "Please, let me finish."

"What about Mother? Rosemary asked, her eyes filling with tears.

"Please, let me finish and then I'll answer your questions the best I can." He took a deep breath and waited a few moments before he continued. "The scooter was found in the Crawfish River. There is no sign of Tillie and the search party has split into two groups. One group is searching upstream and the other downstream. So far, nothing more has been found. We aren't even sure she is in that area, but we will continue the search until we either find her or rule it out."

"Where in the Crawfish?" Joseph asked.

"The scooter was found off Lewis Street, across from the cemetery. I believe the area would be about where the city limits end."

"That can't be right," Rosemary said, still holding Joseph's hand. "She doesn't know anyone that far up the road. There isn't any reason that she would have been up there." She pulled her hand away and stood up. "No. She wouldn't have been up there. Mother always stays on the sidewalks unless she has to cross the street. She wouldn't go where she had to ride on the road." She started pacing back and forth, trying to get her thoughts together. "I'm sorry,

Sergeant Haase, but if Tillie's scooter was found in the river, someone dumped it there."

"There are sidewalks there, you know," Haase commented. "She could have stayed on the sidewalks."

"What difference does it make?" Lynn exclaimed. "Grams' scooter may be there, but Grams isn't. You need to widen the search."

"Lynn, believe me, everyone is doing their best."

"And, I appreciate it. However, we don't need a babysitter here and the people searching could probably use your help."

"Are you kicking me out?" Haase asked Lynn.

"I'm sorry. Of course, I'm not kicking you out. But I would like you to go look over the area where they found the scooter and, then, come back and tell us what you think. I'd rather have the information firsthand from you."

"I would do that, but I've been asked to stay here and I don't have a whole lot of choices."

"Asked or ordered?" Lynn inquired.

"It's one and the same," Haase told her.

"Well, I've asked you and now I'm ordering you," Lynn told him. "Please, go take a look."

Sergeant Haase held back a smile, knowing how serious the situation was. "I'm sorry, Lynn, but I can't. I'll check with the Chief and see if there's any more news. That's the best I can do right now."

"Lynn, quit picking on the man," Joseph said. "He has orders and he has to follow them."

"Well, fine," Lynn said, in a huff. "Let him stay here. But, there's nothing to keep me from going up there and finding out what's going on."

"Oh, I'm sorry, but I'm afraid I can't let you do that," Haase told her.

"And, why not? Am I under house arrest or something?"

"Of course, you're not under arrest. But that area is considered an active crime scene right now. You won't be allowed on it. You'd be wasting your time and I was asked to make sure you all stay here."

Lynn looked at him, shaking her head from side to side. "Asked or ordered?"

Sergeant Haase turned away so she couldn't see him grinning.

"Who ordered what?" Stacy asked, as the door swung open and she walked in. "I sure hope it was pizza. I'm starving."
"

Twenty-four

Chief Daniel Austin watched while Officer Benisch, whose duties included being the police photographer, finished taking pictures of the area where the scooter was found. "Did you get good shots of the tire tracks?" Austin asked Benisch.

"I did. Anything else you need here?"

"Nope." Austin looked over at Officer Gorski, who was searching through the long grass. "Bob," he called out.

Officer Gorski straightened up and stretched. "What?"

"I want casts of those tire tracks."

"Gotcha. Both sets, right?" Gorski inquired.

"Both sets."

Austin watched as the scooter was pushed up the hill to the road. A tow truck was waiting to load it and take it back to the station. Once there, it would be examined for any evidence that might remain after being in the river for almost twenty-four hours.

"Do you think you'll find anything?" Joe, the truck driver, asked him.

"Not really, but we still have to try," Austin told him.

"Shame about the old lady," Joe commented.

"Don't get ahead of yourself," Austin said. "We don't know where she is or what has happened. She's not dead yet."

As Joe started pushing the scooter up the ramp onto the back of the tow truck, he pulled his hand away. "Did you see this?" he called over to Austin.

"What's that?"

"It looks like the back of this thing was hit by something. It's got one hell of a big dent here."

Austin walked over to the back of the truck and looked at the scooter. "You're right. It looks like it might have been hit by a car. See here, where the paint is scraped off? That could have been done by a car hitting it."

"Or, a truck, maybe," Joe added.

"Well, if it was hit, let's hope there was a transfer of paint by the vehicle that hit it. Handle that scooter with kid gloves, Joe."

"Will do. By the way, is this Red?"

Chief Austin smiled. "It sure is."

"Man," Joe said. "I've heard a million stories about this scooter."

"And, most of them are probably true," Austin told him. "Tillie has had a ball on that thing."

"Yup. I heard. What a way to go."

"Come on, Joe. I told you, we don't know Tillie's status."

"Oh, I know that," Joe said. "I meant the scooter, not Tillie."

Once darkness set in, Chief Austin decided to call it quits for the day. He glanced over at Officer Gorski, who was walking towards his squad car. "Bob, would you ask everyone to meet down at the station? Let them know that there is food waiting for them courtesy of Rahn's Deli. Also, thank the volunteers for their help today. Let them know how much we all appreciate it. I know most of these people have to work tomorrow, but we need to resume the search for Tillie early in the morning. Will you find out if any of them can help out again?"

"Sure thing, Chief."

"You know there are a lot of teenagers not doing anything this summer. Check with the parents that are helping search for Tillie and see if they have any kids that can help out. Okay?"

"Got it. What time do you plan on starting in the morning?" Gorski asked.

"Around five or so, I guess. See if they can be at the station between five and six."

"Where are you off to?"

Chief Austin frowned. "I'm going to go talk with Tillie's daughter and husband. My gut is telling me that something is off with them."

"Like what?"

"It's just a feeling, but every time Tillie has been missing, even if it's just for a couple of hours, Rosemary calls and reports it. Yet, this time, she waited over ten hours. I want to know why?"

Officer Gorski shrugged his shoulders. "It does seem a little strange. What time did they notice she was missing?"

"Rosemary said it was sometime after two-thirty yesterday. However, they did think that she might have been riding around on her scooter. But, when Tillie wasn't home by dark, I would think Rosemary would have called us then."

"It definitely sounds suspicious," Gorski agreed.

"It does and I need to go check it out. As soon as you're done talking to the volunteers, head home and get some rest, Bob. The sun will be up before you know it."

Chief Daniel Austin was the third generation of Austins to work his way up the ranks and become the top cop of the Columbus Police Force. Most of the time he loved his job, but tonight he wished he was anyplace except here, sitting in his squad car in front of Rosemary and Joseph Larson's house. He sighed, as he opened the car door, exited his squad, and walked to their front door.

The door opened before he had a chance to ring the bell. "Did you find her?" Rosemary exclaimed.

Austin shook his head no. "Sorry, no. I need to talk to you and Joe, though. Is he still up?"

"Come on in," Rosemary said. "He's in the living room."

"Who else is here?"

"All of our children are here. Simon is at home with the grandkids."

"Is Sergeant Haase still here?" Austin asked.

"I believe he's in the kitchen, talking to Lynn," Rosemary told him. "What's going on, Daniel?"

"Excuse me, Rosemary, but I need to talk to the Sergeant for a moment."

"What is it?" Joseph asked. "Did you find something?"

"Just give me a few minutes. I'll be right back."

Austin walked into the kitchen, opened the back door, and motioned for Sergeant Haase to join him. "You need to get back to the station, but before you go, I need to talk to you."

"Outside?" Haase asked.

"Outside."

"Has anyone said anything that sounds a little off?" Austin asked Haase, as soon as they were outside standing on the driveway.

Sergeant Haase thought for a moment and, then, shook his head no. "There's nothing I can think of. Why?"

"It looks like Tillie's scooter was hit in the rear end by something. We'll be checking it out, of course, but I want you to take a look at Joseph's and Rosemary's cars and see if there are any dents or scratches on the front bumpers."

Haase stared at Austin, a shocked look on his face. "You're not serious? do you think that Rosemary or Joseph had something to do with Tillie disappearing?

"I didn't say that. But you know as well as I do that, nine times out of ten, it's family when something like this happens."

"You think she's dead?"

"Right now, Matt, I don't know what to think. I only know that until we find her, everyone is suspect. And, that includes her family."

"Well, you can rule out Lynn and Stacy. Lynn was working in Madison until after six. Stacy was with Simon and the kids shopping in Beaver Dam. I'm not sure about Junior."

"What time did he get here?"

"Junior? I guess it was around four or so," Haase told him.

"That's about right. When I found out he was part of the search party, I had him sent home. I told him his parents needed him at their house with them."

"Well, if he's a suspect, he can't be out there searching and possibly destroying any evidence he finds," Haase declared.

"I doubt he had anything to do with this," Austin commented, "but until I'm sure . . ." He looked away and let out a deep breath. "Well, you know."

"You want me to check out the cars now?" Sergeant Haase asked.

"Go see if the side door to the garage is open," Austin told him.

Austin watched while Haase walked over to the side of the garage and tried to open the door. Finding the door unlocked, Haase turned and gave his boss a thumbs up, and entered the garage.

Austin waited until he saw Haase's flashlight come on and, then, walked over to the garage door and looked in. "I'm going back in the house," he told Haase. "Text me immediately if you find anything."

Twenty-five

"Did Matt leave?" Lynn asked, as soon as Chief Austin came back into the house.

"I sent him back to the station," Austin told her.

"He could at least have said goodbye."

"He can do his socializing on his own time. Right now, he's working," Austin said. He walked into the living room and looked for a place to sit down.

"Junior, get Chief Austin a chair from the dining room, will you?" Joseph asked his son.

"Sure thing," Junior replied.

Austin waited while Junior brought him a chair. He took his notepad out of his breast pocket and sat down, facing the family.

"Before I start, I want you all to understand that the questions I'm about to ask you are strictly routine. In no way am I pointing a finger at any one of you. But there are a few things, that seem a little off to me, which I need to clear up."

"Like what?" Junior asked.

"Lynn, let's start with you. I understand that you were working at your job in Madison Friday afternoon," he stated, ignoring Junior's question.

"That's correct."

"When was the last time you spoke to your grandmother?" Austin asked her.

"Wednesday night. We talked about going out for dinner on Sunday."

"Do you recall the time?"

Lynn thought for a moment. "I guess it was about seven or so. I know it was after I had finished dinner."

"Did she mention any plans she had for Friday?"

"Like what?"

"Anything at all. Like meeting up with friends or going to lunch with someone."

"No, nothing like that. We mostly talked about what we'd do this weekend after my parents left for their trip."

"Stacy, I understand you were with your husband and children shopping in Beaver Dam on Friday afternoon. Is that correct?"

"It is. We went to lunch first and then to the mall. We figured we'd get a head start on shopping for new school clothes for the kids."

Austin's phone beeped, indicating he had a text. "Excuse me a second." He read the text, typed something, and put the phone back in his pocket.

"Do you recall what time you got home?" Austin continued.

"It was later in the day. After shopping, we went to the show and that didn't get out until around five-thirty or six."

"Do you recall the last time you spoke to Tillie?" Austin asked her.

"On Thursday morning. I called and asked how her friends were doing. You know, the ones that got hurt in that stupid accident downtown."

"Do you recall what time you talked to her?" Austin asked.

"It was kind of early. Probably around nine or so," Stacy told him.

"Did she mention anything about plans for

Friday?"

"Not to me."

"Thank you." Austin made a few notes and turned his attention to Joseph Junior. "Where were you on Friday, Junior?"

"Not here making grandma disappear," he answered sarcastically.

"Junior!" Rosemary exclaimed. "That's a horrible thing to say."

"Well, obviously he thinks one of us did something to her. Why else would he be asking these questions?"

"He already told us these were routine questions, you dick head!" Lynn yelled.

"Enough," Austin said. "Where were you, Junior?"

"I was getting on a plane in Chicago. I spent Wednesday and Thursday there on business and left Friday morning to come home."

"You live in Beaver Dam, right?" Austin asked him.

"That's right."

"Did you fly into Madison from Chicago?"

"I did."

"How did you get from Madison to Beaver Dam?" Austin asked him.

"I drove. My car was parked at the airport in Madison."

"What time did you get home?"

"Around two o'clock, I guess."

"Did you stop anywhere between Madison and your house?" Austin asked him.

183

"No. And, I hadn't talked to Grandma since our luncheon last Sunday, so I don't know if she had any plans for Friday," Junior told Austin.

Chief Austin made a few more notes and cleared his throat. "I hate to bother you, but could I get a glass of water?"

"I'll get it for you," Stacy said.

"Thank you."

"Are you done with me?" Junior asked. "I need to get home."

"You what?" Joseph exclaimed.

"I'm sorry, Dad, but there's nothing I can do here and I've got a ton of paperwork waiting for me at home."

"I thought you were going to spend the night here," Rosemary commented.

"I'll be back first thing in the morning. Okay?" Junior looked at Austin. "Can I leave or not?"

"I don't see why not. If I need to talk to you again, I'll get in touch."

"Chief Austin is going to fill us in about what he found today," Rosemary told Junior. "Don't you want to stay and hear what he has to say?"

"You can tell me tomorrow," Junior said, as he got up and walked to the door. "Oh, but call me if they find Grandma. Good night, everyone."

Rosemary glanced over at Austin with a shocked look on her face. "I'm sorry. I've never seen him act like that before. He was downright rude. I apologize for his behavior."

Austin took the glass of water from Stacy and took a long swallow. "Thank you." He looked at the coffee table. "Do I need a coaster?"

"What?" Rosemary asked, looking confused.

"For the glass," Austin replied. "Do I need to use a coaster?"

"It's fine. Just put it down," Joseph said. "Now, what news do you have about Tillie?"

"In a minute. First, I have a couple of questions for you and Rosemary."

Joseph sighed. "Go ahead."

"You worked until what time on Friday?"

"I think it was around one o'clock."

"Where did you go after you left work?" Austin asked him.

"I came straight home. I had some packing to do for our trip."

"Rosemary said you came in the house about two-thirty. It takes about ten minutes for you to drive home. Where were you the rest of the time?" Austin inquired.

"I was pulling weeds. When I pulled into the driveway, I noticed that some of the flower beds needed some attention, so I just started pulling weeds. I didn't want to be gone for a couple of weeks and let those weeds get totally out of hand. They'll take over if you don't stay on top of them, you know."

"So, you pulled weeds for over an hour? Is that correct?"

"I guess that sounds about right."

"And, Rosemary didn't know you were here?" Austin inquired.

"I guess not. I know I scared her when I came into the house."

"Rosemary, you were in the kitchen part of the time that Joseph was outside doing yard work. Didn't you notice his car in the driveway?"

"Of course, she didn't," Joseph answered. "I put the car in the garage."

"Were you home all day on Friday?" Austin asked Rosemary.

"All day."

"You didn't run out to the store to do any last-minute shopping?"

Rosemary looked concerned. "I don't understand why you're asking me all these questions. I already told you that I was here all day."

"Don't get upset," Austin said. "We're almost done here. You said that you thought Tillie was taking a nap when Joseph got home. But her scooter was gone and so was she. Isn't it a little strange that she would just leave the house and not say anything to you?"

"Joseph, why is he asking me all these questions?" Rosemary looked at her husband, tears starting to roll down her cheeks.

Joseph stared at Austin. "Can we finish this up, please? You're really upsetting Rosemary."

"And, I'm sorry for that. I'm just about done."

Stacy, who was sitting across the room from Lynn listening to the conversation, feigned a cough. As Lynn glanced over at her, she mouthed the words *what the fuck?"*

Lynn shrugged, indicating that she didn't know.

Austin turned to Stacy "I saw that. What you need to understand is that we are dealing with a missing person. The sooner I get answers the better our chances of finding her."

"We understand that, Chief Austin," Stacy said. "It's just that Mother has been through a lot today and her nerves are shot."

Austin shook his head. "You're absolutely right. She has been and I don't mean to be insensitive. Unfortunately, when things like this happen, I need to ask questions that might seem unsympathetic or unfeeling. But, believe me, I feel for all of you and what you're going through. So, please, just bear with me. I'm just about done here." He reached down for the glass and took another swallow of water. "Did Tillie ever mention that her scooter had any damage to it?"

No one said a word. Austin waited a few moments. "Was Tillie's scooter ever hit by a car?"

No one said a word. "When we pulled the scooter out of the river, we noticed that the back of it had some scratches and dents. Do you know if those were there before Friday?"

"Oh, my god. You actually think someone ran over Grams," Lynn exclaimed.

"I didn't say that," Austin said.

"Rosemary," Joseph said softly. "Do you want to tell him?"

Rosemary put her face in her hands, crying. "I'm so ashamed."

"What is it, Joseph?" Austin asked.

Joseph pursed his lips and let out a deep sigh. "It's nothing to do with this at all. Everyone knows that Rosemary has never been happy with Tillie having that scooter. It's been the cause of many fights and

Rosemary is worried sick every time Tillie takes off on that thing."

"Just remember that it was you who thought it was a good idea for her to get it," Rosemary exclaimed. "If you had backed me up, none of this would be going on now."

"Please, Rosemary, let Joseph finish," Austin said.

"Plain and simple. Rosemary took a hammer to it a few weeks ago. She was upset and rather than get into a big fight with Tillie, she took her anger out on Red."

Stacy glanced over at Lynn, who was fighting to hold back a smile. *Stop it,* she mouthed and looked away.

Austin sat back in his chair, surprised at what Joseph had just told him. "I see. Well, I guess that clears up that mystery."

"Mother was so mad at me when she saw that scooter. I told her I'd get it fixed; that I'd pay for it. But she told me she didn't want my damn money. She said that she had enough of her own money to buy ten or twenty scooters. After that, she never mentioned it again," Rosemary said.

"Does Tillie still have Lowell's old car?" Austin asked, changing the topic of conversation.

"No. She sold it to a guy I work with," Joseph told him.

"So, you just have the two cars? The Buick and the Toyota?"

"That's right," Joseph replied.

"Who drives the Buick?"

"Mostly Rosemary, but we switch off occasionally."

"I don't like driving the Highlander," Rosemary commented. "It's too big, so I only drive it if I have to."

"All right. I'm about done here. I know it's late and you guys need to get some rest."

"I don't think any of us will get much rest tonight, Chief," Lynn said.

"Probably not." Austin looked down at his notes for a moment. "Just one last thing," he said, looking over at Rosemary. "Tell me, Rosemary. Why did you wait over ten hours before calling the police to report that Tillie was missing?" Austin asked.

The minute Austin left the Larson's home, he called Sergeant Haase. "Are you still at the station?" Austin asked as he drove out of the driveway.

"I am."

"So, the Buick has a few scratches on the front bumper?"

"It does. I took some pictures of it. I also took pictures of the tires on both cars. I think you should get a warrant so we can check them out a little more. I didn't see any red paint on the bumper, but it was kind of dark in there."

"Good. Go on home. There's nothing more we can do here tonight. I have some things we need to check out. I'll go over them with you tomorrow. Also, I want you to contact the people that were with Tillie on Wednesday when they had that accident. Ask them if they remember seeing dents and scratches on the back of Tillie's scooter. She was leading the way, so if they

189

were with her on Wednesday, they would have seen them."

"Will do. Did you get any more information from the family?"

"Not really. That Junior is a strange one, though. He couldn't wait to get out of there and go home."

"Did Lynn stay there or go home?"

Austin smiled. "She's still there."

"Do you think it's too late to give her a call?"

Twenty-six

The second pot of coffee was already brewing when Chief Austin walked into the police station. "Smells good," he muttered to himself. He looked around the room and saw Sergeant Wong opening a box of donuts. "What time did you get in?" Austin asked.

"Around five," Wong told him. "I got a couple of jelly donuts for you, so you better grab them now before the rest of the crew gets here."

"Thanks, Lee, but I need coffee more than donuts right now. Did you get much sleep?"

"A few hours, I guess. I could have used more. This is going to be a long day."

"You can say that again." Austin poured a cup of coffee and sat down at his desk. "I've got a list of things that need to be checked out today. How about you stay here and take care of them before you join in the search?"

"Fine with me," Wong replied. "What are they?"

"I think it's obvious that a car parked on the side of the hill and unloaded the scooter. You could see the marks the scooter made as it was pushed into the river. We need to get those casts made as soon as possible."

"I think that has been done already," Wong said. "Gorski did that yesterday."

Austin thought for a moment. "That's right."

"What else do you need?" Wong asked.

"Track down the people that were with Tillie when they piled up the other day on James Street. Ask them if any of them noticed that the back of Tillie's scooter was dented and had scratches on it. And, remind me to tell Matt that you're doing this, not him."

"He was going to do it?" Wong asked.

"I mentioned it last night, but I want him in the field today. Also, find out what time Junior Larson's plane left Chicago and landed in Madison on Friday. And, check with airport parking to find out how long his car was parked there."

"Got it." Wong looked at Austin. "You think the family is involved in this?"

"I'm just covering all the bases," Austin told him. "I want you to check with Joseph Larson's boss and find out what time he left work on Friday."

Sergeant Wong waited while Chief Austin flipped through his notes.

"Is that it?" Wong asked.

"For now," Austin told him. Hearing voices coming from the hall, he walked over to the table, grabbed the two jelly donuts and a napkin, and walked back to his desk. "Looks like we're going to get an early start," he said.

The knocking on the door woke Joseph Larson. He glanced over at the clock and noticed that it was already seven-thirty. He grabbed his robe, putting it on as he walked into the living room to answer the door.

"Dad, I'll get it," Lynn said, as she walked towards the door.

Joseph looked at his daughter, who was already dressed and holding a cup of coffee. He watched as she swung the door open.

192

"Do you ever sleep?" Lynn said as she stepped aside to make room for Austin to enter the living room.

"I could say the same for you," Austin told her. "Good morning, Joseph."

"Daniel," Joseph said, acknowledging him. "Is there any news?"

"Sorry, but nothing yet. We had a good turnout of volunteers this morning. Let's hope we find Tillie today."

"Coffee, Chief?" Lynn asked.

"I'm good, thanks."

"Dad?"

"What?"

"Do you want some coffee?"

"I'll get it," Joseph told her.

"Where is the search party going to be looking today?" Lynn asked.

"We're checking the river, going south from where we found the scooter. We also have a canine unit coming up from Madison."

Lynn sighed. "Do you think Grams is dead?"

Chief Austin frowned. "Right now, Lynn, we are working under the assumption that she is still alive. She may be hurt somewhere and needs help."

"But you've got dogs coming and you're . . ."

"Lynn, stop imagining things. We use dogs every day to find people. Living people."

"I'm sorry. It's just that we're all going nuts trying to figure out what happened."

"Just hang in there. Is your mom here?" Austin asked.

"No. She went to church to pray," Lynn replied.

"A lot of good that's gonna do," Joseph said. "Of course, she prayed every day that Tillie's scooter would disappear and it did, so maybe somebody up there is actually listening."

"Dad!"

"I'm sorry, Lynn, but it's true. The day that she got that damn scooter our lives changed. Your mother hated it and Tillie did everything she could to aggravate her. There were times when your mother thought Tillie was trying to drive her crazy."

"You don't think Rosemary would have done anything to her, do you?" Austin asked Joseph.

"What?" Joseph replied, a shocked look on his face. "Of course, not. My god, Dan, that's a horrible thing to say."

"I need to take a look at your cars, Joseph," Austin stated.

Joseph looked confused. "What are you talking about?"

"Just what I said. I need to take a look at your cars. Do I have your permission to go into your garage?"

"What do you think you're going to find?"

"For starters, I understand that there is a scratch on the Buick's front bumper. I need to take a look at it," Austin answered.

"It's not here. Rosemary drove it to church. Go look at it there if you want to see it." Joseph shook his head in disgust. "My god, that car is almost four years old. It stands to reason that it may have some bumps and bruises. What now? You think one of us hit that damn scooter?"

"Anything is possible, Joseph."

"Well, well, well. Is this what it's come to, Daniel? You can't find Tillie, so now the family is under suspicion?"

"You have to understand that I have to check everything out, even if that includes you and your family."

"We don't even know if she's alive or dead and you're already concluding that one of us killed her," Joseph said, sarcastically.

Austin sighed. "No, I'm not. I'm just doing what I need to do. If anything, this will clear you of suspicion."

Joseph stared at him. "Do what you need to do," he snapped. "Just get the hell out of my house and leave us alone, will you?"

"Thank you." Austin turned and looked at Lynn. "Would you mind opening the garage door?"

Lynn pointed to the garage door opener on the wall by the kitchen's back door. "Help yourself," she said, not moving.

"And, don't come back until you have some news about Tillie," Joseph yelled, as Austin walked out of the back door.

It only took Austin a few minutes to realize that the tires on the Highlander were not a match to the tire marks they saw on the hill. As he got into his vehicle to leave, he thought about driving over to the Catholic Church to see if Rosemary was still there. As he started to pull out of the driveway, his phone rang. He glanced at the caller I.D., saw that it was Sergeant

Wong, and answered the call. "Whataya got, Lee?"

"A couple of things. I talked to three of Tillie's scooter friends and none of them remember seeing any damage to the back of her scooter. Of course, two out of the three are half-blind, so I can't rely on their statements. The third one, Minnie Williams, who is in the hospital, can see pretty well and she emphatically states that there were no dents or scratches there on Wednesday."

"Well, that's interesting," Austin commented. "What else?"

"Joseph was off a little on the time he left work on Friday. His boss says it was more like noon, not one o'clock."

"Well, so far, that's two out of three misstatements. Did you find out anything about Junior?"

"I did, and you're three for three, Chief. I can't find any record of Junior flying in or out of O'Hare any day last week."

Chief Austin thought for a moment. "You know there's more than one airport in Chicago. Did you try the other one? You know . . . What the hell is the name of that place?"

"Midway," Wong told him.

"Right. Check that one out, too. And, check with the Madison airport to see if he arrived on any flight last Friday."

"I should have done that. Sorry. Once, I found out that he didn't fly out of O'Hare, I just assumed he was lying. I didn't follow through."

"Don't sweat it, Lee. Just check it out. Okay?"

196

"Will do. I'll get back to you on that. Are you still at Larson's?"

"I'm sitting in their driveway."

"Do the tires match up?" Wong asked Austin.

"Not the Toyota. Rosemary's over at her church praying, so I couldn't check her car."

"All right. Anything else for me?"

"Not right now. Whoa. Guess who's home?"

"Rosemary," Wong said.

"You got it. I'll talk to you later."

Chief Austin pulled his car out of the driveway and parked in front of the Larson house. He waited until Rosemary pulled into the garage before he got out of his car.

"Rosemary," he yelled, as she started to exit the garage. "Don't shut the garage door."

Rosemary looked at him and frowned. "Do you have any news?" she inquired, as he walked towards her.

"Sorry, no. But there are almost a hundred men out searching for her right now."

"Well, why are you here? Shouldn't you be out looking for my mother, too?"

"I need to take a look at your car." Austin walked by her and went into the garage. He bent down and looked at the tires on Rosemary's Buick. He reached for his phone and snapped a couple of pictures of the tires, already knowing that they weren't a match. He walked to the front of the car and checked out the bumper. "Looks like you have some damage here," he mentioned, as he took a few more pictures.

"Really?" Rosemary inquired. "I don't remember

197

doing anything to cause that. Maybe, Joseph. . ." She stopped talking and frowned. "Oh, my. Joseph's going to be so mad."

"Why's that?" Austin asked.

"A few days ago, when I pulled into the garage, I went a little too far and hit the workbench. I didn't think I had hit it hard enough to do any damage, so I didn't even take a look at the bumper." She glanced over at the car and, then, back at Austin. "Don't say anything to Joseph. Okay?"

Austin looked confused. "Why wouldn't you tell him?"

"This will be the third time I've done that. I'll tell him eventually, but now isn't a good time." Rosemary smiled at him. "Please, Daniel?"

Austin shook his head. "Okay, I'll leave it up to you to tell him. But I am going to have someone else take a look at that damage." He turned and started to walk back to his squad car.

"Why? I just told you what happened."

"There are scratches on the back of Tillie's scooter and on your front bumper. We have to make sure. . ."

"That it wasn't my car that damaged her scooter?" Rosemary interrupted. "Is that what you're getting at?"

"Sorry, Rosemary. It has to be checked."

"I would never hurt my mother," Rosemary told him, as she started to cry.

"Sorry, Rosemary. I have to leave," he said, as he walked towards his car.

"Daniel?"

Austin turned and looked at her. "Yes?"

"Do you think you'll ever find my mother?"

"I do."

Twenty-seven

"Junior Larson flew out of Midway," Sergeant Wong told Austin. "His times are pretty accurate, so I guess he was driving home when Tillie went missing."

"True. But we don't know if he bypassed Columbus and went straight home to Beaver Dam. Let's see if we can get someone to verify what time he got home. Check with his neighbors and see if any of them saw anything."

"Right."

"Also, Lee, check around and see if any of the auto stores around here sold a set of tires to Joseph Larson recently."

Wong looked slightly confused. "A set of tires?"

"The Highlander has brand new tires on it. They look like they have only been on the car a couple of days."

"Do you think that Joseph put new tires on that car since Friday?"

"I don't know. If he did, I don't know when he would have done it. But I still need to check it out." Austin glanced over at the coffee pot, noticed that it was half full, and grabbed his cup."

"You keep drinking that stuff, you're gonna be climbing the walls," Wong said, grinning.

"You're probably right, but I need to stay awake."

"Have you heard anything from the search parties?"

"They checked in about an hour ago. So far, nothing."

"What's your vibe on this, Chief?" Wong asked.

"The chances of finding Tillie alive get slimmer by the hour. So, right now, I'd say it's not looking good."

Austin sat back in his chair, put his feet up on his desk, and stared at the ceiling. "You know . . ."

Wong glanced over at him. "What?"

"Nothing. It's just this feeling I've got." Austin dropped his feet to the floor and stood up. "Call Judge Maxwell and tell him you're on your way over to see him. I want a search warrant for those two cars."

"What about me finding out if Larson bought tires?

"Get Cynthia to do it. She's not doing anything right now except answering the phone," Austin replied. "Okay. I'm out of here. Call me when you get back with that warrant."

"Where are you going?"

"To check with Haase and Gorski and see how the search is going."

"I seriously don't know where else to look," Haase told Chief Austin. "We've covered everything from where the scooter went into the water to here," he said, indicating the river behind the Columbus Antique Mall. "We're going to need divers for this area."

"I'll contact the State Police and see if they have some divers they can send over. I doubt it will be before tomorrow, though. We've only got a few more hours of daylight."

"So, what do you want us to do?" Haase asked.

"Call it a day," Austin said. "Everyone's tired,

and I'd like to have their help again tomorrow. We should start searching the cemeteries and the fields near to where we think Tillie disappeared."

"Should I contact Gorski and let him know?" Haase asked.

Austin held up his finger, indicating for Haase to wait a moment. He pulled out his phone and took a call. "Austin."

"I've got the warrant," Wong told him.

"I'll be right there," Austin said. He hung up the call and looked at Haase. "Wrap this up, will you? I've got a warrant to serve."

"For god's sake, Chief Austin, you didn't need to get a warrant. All you had to do was ask," Lynn declared.

"I did ask. Your father said no."

"You have to understand how upset he is. It's already Monday and Grams has been missing since Friday. We don't have one clue as to what may have happened to her. And, now you come over here acting like he's a suspect or something. Maybe, if I was in his position, I would have said no, too."

"I'm sorry, Lynn. Now, if you'll excuse me, I've got work to do. I'm going to have to ask you to go back to the house."

"I want to watch and see what you're doing in the garage," Lynn retorted.

"Nope. Afraid that isn't going to happen. Now, in the house with you."

Lynn gave him a defiant look and didn't move.

"Go or I'll have one of my officers carry you in,"

Austin told her.

Lynn stared at him and, then, smiled. "All right. I choose Matt."

"For what?" Austin said, confused.

"To carry me into the house. I choose Matt."

Austin grinned. "Very funny. Now get out of here."

Sergeant Haase, Sergeant Wong, and Chief Austin watched the garage door go up. Haase looked around his surroundings and sighed. "Where do you want us to start?" he asked Austin.

"Check the workbench and the tools. See if there is a hammer or some tool that was used to make those dents in Tillie's scooter. Check for red paint. Also, check the front of the Buick and see if there is any transfer paint on the bumper. If those scratches were made by that car hitting the back of the scooter, there may be some red paint on it."

"Do you want me to check the inside of the vehicles?" Wong asked.

"We can't. The warrant is limited to anything that is in sight," Austin said.

"Well, the car is in sight, isn't it?"

"You can look through the windows, but we can't go inside. We barely got the warrant for searching the garage with practically no evidence. Let's not blow it."

Sergeant Haase walked over to the workbench and started checking the tools. He picked up a hammer, shined his flashlight on it, and checked it out. Nothing. He continued to examine every tool that was hanging on the wall, looking for a trace of red paint. When he finished with those, he opened a toolbox and looked inside. He lifted the tray out and found a large wrench, covered with a rag at the bottom of the box. As he unwrapped the wrench, he saw what looked like rust on it and immediately laid it back down on the rag. "Chief," he called out. "I may have found something."

Austin walked over to Haase and looked down at the wrench. "Is this what you're talking about?" he asked, pointing at the tool.

"Do you think that's blood?" Haase asked.

"It could be, I guess," Austin said.

"Should I bag it?

"Definitely. We need to have it analyzed."

Thirty minutes later, Austin knocked on the back door of the Larson house. Lynn opened the door and invited him in.

"What is it now?" Joseph yelled from the living room.

"I just want to let you know that we finished up in the garage," Austin told him.

"Fine. Anything else you need?" Joseph asked him.

"I'd like to have something that has Tillie's DNA on it. Would you have a hairbrush of hers that I could take with me?"

"Oh, my god," Rosemary exclaimed. "Did you find her? Is she dead?"

"No, no, Rosemary. I didn't mean to scare you. But, just in case we find anything. . . You know, evidence or something. . . Well, we'll have a sample of her DNA."

"Oh, dear God," Lynn uttered under her breath. "What next?"

Joseph, who had been sitting in the living room watching TV, suddenly stood up and walked into the kitchen. "Didn't find anything, did you?" he snapped.

Austin didn't reply.

"I don't know why you're bound and determined to make me the bad guy, Austin. But I didn't have anything to do with this."

Austin sighed. "Joseph, I never said you did. You know I have a job to do and this is part of it. Everything that we're doing here will simply cross you off the list. But we have to consider everyone as suspects right now. I'm sorry if all of this offends you, but that's just the way it is." He glanced over at Lynn. "Hairbrush?"

"Hold on," Lynn said. "I'll get it for you."

Twenty-eight

"I don't friggin' believe it."

Chief Austin glanced over at Sergeant Haase. "You don't believe what?"

"That was forensics that just called. It definitely is blood on the wrench and it's been there for a while."

"So, it's not Tillie's blood?"

"Nope. The blood was a match to Lowell Dobson. It looks like we finally found what was used to kill him," Haase told him.

Austin shook his head, agreeing with Haase. "And, maybe we also found our murderer."

"Joseph Larson? You think he killed Lowell?"

"His wrench, right?"

"I suppose so. It was found in his garage. But there aren't any prints on it. Right now, anyone with access to it could have done it."

"Do you want to take a ride?" Austin asked him.

"To the Larson's?"

"Yup. Let's go see what Joseph has to say about this."

"It's not mine," Joseph said, smirking. "I don't know where you found it, but it doesn't belong to me."

"It was in your toolbox in your garage, Joseph."

"What?" Suddenly, Joseph laughed. "Really, Dan, it isn't mine. That was Lowell's toolbox. A lot of the stuff in the garage was Lowell's. If that wrench has Lowell's blood on it, it was there before we ever moved here."

Austin sighed. "Well, if that's true, then, that's

good news. I have to say, I'm relieved that the wrench isn't yours."

"No problem, Dan. You're just doing your job. Right?" Joseph commented, still smiling.

"Is Lynn here?" Sergeant Haase asked.

"Nah, she had to go to work. I think she'll be back here around six or so."

"I'm surprised she didn't stay around," Austin commented.

"She has a mortgage payment and bills to pay. Like I said, she'll be back here tonight," Joseph said. "Is there anything else you need?"

On Tuesday night, Chief Austin called off the search for Tillie. The divers had not found a body, the canines never picked up Tillie's scent, and the fields and woods surrounding the town had been thoroughly searched. Austin thanked everyone for their help and waited until everyone, except his team, had left the building. He sat down at his desk and started going through his notes one more time. He was just about to call it quits and go home when the phone rang.

"Police Department," Austin heard Haase say. He glanced over at his Sergeant and listened, wondering if it was bad news and they'd have to go out on a call.

"Of course, I know who you are, Mrs. Yerges," Haase said. "Okay. Rose, it is. Now?" He listened for a few moments, and, then, looked over at Austin. "We got something," he mouthed.

"What?" Austin asked.

"No, that's not a problem. We'll be there in a few

minutes. No, thank you, Rose."

Sergeant Haase ended the call and grinned. "We might just have a break. Rose Yerges says she saw a car parked across from the cemetery last Thursday night."

"Thursday? You mean Friday, don't you?"

"She said Thursday," Haase replied.

"Then, why the hell did she wait until now to call us?" Austin stood up, grabbed his hat, and headed for the door. "You coming?" he shouted.

"Right behind you," Haase yelled back.

Rose Yerges was old. No one knew her exact age. She had lived in Columbus all of her life and was known as the town busybody. Somehow, she managed to know everything that went on in town, even though she rarely left her house. She lived in an old house, across the road and just up from where the scooter had been found. Although her house needed a coat of fresh paint, Rose's flower gardens were beautiful and obviously tended to regularly.

Austin pulled up in front of her house and looked around. "Ready?" he asked Haase.

"I'm ready." Suddenly, he sat back in his seat and looked at Austin. "You know, why don't I just wait for you here?"

"Get your ass out of the car, you chicken shit," Austin said, laughing. "I'm not about to face that woman by myself."

"Then, I guess that makes you chicken shit, too," Haase said. Grinning, Haase joined Austin as he walked to Rose's front door. The door swung open before they had a chance to ring the bell.

"Been watching for ya. The damn bell don't work. Come on in before the mosquitoes eat you alive," Rose ordered.

"Hello, Rose," Austin said. "How are you?"

"I'm doing fine." She glanced over at Haase. "You're the young man I talked to on the telephone. Right?"

"That's right, Rose," Austin said. "This is Sergeant Matt Haase."

"I know who he is," Rose exclaimed. "I know who everybody is in this town."

"Sorry, I forgot that for a moment," Austin said, smiling. "So, what have you got for me?"

"I've been out of town since Friday. I just got back today and I heard about Tillie. Is it really true? Her missing, I mean?"

"Yes, she's missing. She hasn't been seen since Friday afternoon."

"Ah-huh."

Austin looked at her.

"Well, what else?" Rose inquired.

Austin looked confused. "What else? Well, we called off the search tonight. Rose, we haven't a clue as to where she might be."

"And, Red? I understand you found him across the road over there in the river. Is that right?"

"That's right. We found the scooter on Saturday," Austin told her, wondering where this was going.

"Well, it took you long enough to find it."

"I don't know what you're getting at. We didn't

even know Tillie was missing until early Saturday morning."

"I'd offer you some coffee, but it's too late for coffee. Would you like a beer?"

Haase glanced over at Austin. "You know what, Rose? I'm off duty. I'm just here to keep the Chief company. I'd love a beer."

Rose stood up, opened the refrigerator, and took out three beers. She handed one to each of the men, took the cap off her beer, and took a sip. She glanced at Austin. "You're off duty, too, Daniel."

Austin grinned and popped the cap. "Thanks," he said and took a long swallow. "That hits the spot."

"So, Mrs. Yerges, what . . ."

"Rose. I told you to call me Rose," she said, interrupting Sergeant Haase.

"Sorry, Rose. What have you got for us?"

"I don't sleep a lot. Many nights I sit in the dark and stare out the front window. There isn't a whole lot of traffic on this road late at night, but there are always a few cars or trucks going by. Last Thursday night, I saw a . . ." Rose hesitated. "What do they call those big cars?"

"You mean an SUV?" Haase replied.

"That's it. An SUV. Anyway, I saw one of those parked across the street. It sat there for a little while, and then drove a little way down the hill and stopped. Two people got out of it. I watched them walk around for a while. It kind of looked like they were arguing. Anyway, they eventually opened up the back of the SUV and pulled something out."

"Could you see what it was?" Austin interrupted.

"Hold on a minute. I'm getting there," Rose said, taking a swallow of her beer. "I couldn't make out what it was, but I figured it was just garbage that they were dumping. And, at that point, I had to tinkle, so I left the room. When I came back, the SUV was gone."

"Are you sure this was on Thursday?" Haase asked.

"Young man, I may be old, but I sure as hell know what day it is. I left on Friday morning and got home today. So, yes, it was definitely Thursday."

"Could you tell what color the car was?" Austin asked, holding his breath.

"It was pretty dark out, but there's a street light a little way from where they pulled off the road. I can't say for sure what color it was, but it was a light color. I'd say white or cream. It could have been a light gray."

"You didn't happen to get a license plate number, did you?" Haase asked her.

Rose stared at him, shaking her head. "You're cut off," she said, laughing.

"Just a couple of things, if you don't mind. Where did you go for five days?" Austin inquired.

"I visited my sister in Manitowoc. My daughter and her husband picked me up and we drove up there. We all stayed there until today. What else do you need to know?"

"I know it's quite a distance to where the car was, but could you make out if the two people you saw were men or women?" Austin asked her.

"I'd be guessing if I tried to answer that."

"Would you recognize the make of the car if you saw a picture?"

211

"I doubt it," Rose said. "I've told you everything I can remember. If anything else comes to mind, I'll call you."

Austin put his notebook in his pocket and reached for his beer.

"Finish it up, will you?" Rose said. "That Joe Kenda guy is on TV and I don't want to miss his show."

"What show is that?' Haase asked her.

"Homicide Hunter," Rose told him. "You guys should watch it sometime. You might learn a thing or two."

Twenty-nine

"The Toyota dealer in Sun Prairie put four new tires on Joseph's car last Friday."

Chief Austin looked up at his clerk. "I'm sorry. Did I just hear you correctly or was I dreaming?"

Cynthia smiled. "There's nothing wrong with your hearing, Chief. And, guess what?"

Austin closed his eyes and sighed. "Do we have to go through this again?"

"Guess," she said. "Come on. Humor me."

"Let me see. You're gonna have another baby."

"Right. And, God's the father."

"Seriously, Cynthia, what else?"

"I talked to the mechanic that did the work. He said that the old tires were still in really good shape. They probably had another ten to fifteen thousand miles on them."

"So, it wasn't necessary to change them out," Austin declared.

"That's what he said."

"Thanks." Austin stood up and grabbed his hat off his desk.

"Where are you going?" Cynthia asked him.

"I'm gonna go take a look at those old tires."

"I don't think so. Larson took the old tires with him."

Austin looked shocked. "Arc you fu . . . Sorry. Are you friggin' kidding me?"

"Nope. And, nice save, by the way. You almost had to put a dollar in the swear jar," Cynthia replied.

Austin sighed. "So, where do you hide tires?" he said.

"What's that, Chief?" Haase asked, looking up from his desk.

"Nothing." Austin sat back in his chair and glanced up at the ceiling. "How much money was Lowell Dobson worth?" Austin asked Sergeant Haase after a few moments.

Haase pursed his lips and thought for a moment. "If I remember correctly, he was worth around two and a half."

"Million?"

"Yeah. I think that was just his investments. You know, like stocks and annuities. I don't think that included his property or savings."

"So, he was worth way over the two and a half million," Austin declared.

"Hell, they aren't even done counting it yet. The attorneys are still finding accounts here and there."

"Which makes Tillie a very wealthy woman."

"It does. What are you getting at?" Haase asked him.

"Let's take a look at what we've got so far," Austin said. "Tillie and Lowell come back from vacation. They are fighting and Tillie says that she is done with him. Joseph and Stacy take Lowell, who is drunk, to his house and put him to bed. We know, for a fact, that his cousin in Florida tried to kill him while he was staying with him. The coroner said that Lowell probably would have died from arsenic poisoning a few days after coming back home. But, before that can happen, the day after he arrives home, he is found dead from blunt force trauma."

"Okay," Haase agreed. "And, there's no clue as to who did it and we don't have a murder weapon. Then, months after he is killed, the supposed murder weapon shows up in a toolbox in Joseph's garage. Joseph denies owning it and we can't prove he does or doesn't. But, according to the coroner, it pretty much matches the wounds on Lowell's head."

"So, did Joseph, who knows that Tillie is the sole beneficiary of Lowell's will, go back to Lowell's house and kill him after Stacy went home and Rosemary and Tillie were sleeping?"

"It could have happened that way, I guess," Haase said. "He goes in the garage, finds the wrench, goes back into the house, which he previously left unlocked, and hits the old guy in the head, killing him."

"And, now, his mother-in-law is a very rich woman," Austin concludes.

"Too bad we can't prove any of this," Haase commented. "By the way, did you ever find out if Junior went straight home from the airport?"

"He did, not that it makes any difference now. We know he was still in Chicago on Thursday, so he's out of the picture."

"I guess," Haase said. "You don't suspect Lynn or Stacy, do you?"

"Nah, they checked out. Lynn was at work all day on Thursday and had dinner with friends that night. Stacy spent most of the day at the park with her kids."

"Of course, Chief, there is still the possibility

that it was a robbery gone bad and Joseph had nothing to do with it," Haase stated.

"You're right. I guess anything is possible, but you know, Tillie was really flaunting that money in Joseph's and Rosemary's faces."

"I heard that after Lowell died and Tillie inherited all that money, she said she planned on spending as much of it as she could before she died," Haase added.

"Who'd you hear that from?"

"Lynn," Haase replied.

"You know, Matt, I think we have enough circumstantial evidence to get an arrest warrant for Joseph and, maybe, even Rosemary."

"Rosemary?" Haase asked.

"She's been lying to us from the beginning. They both have. Tillie disappeared on Thursday, not Friday. Why would Rosemary lie about when her mother disappeared?" Austin said. "My god, I hate to even think it, much less say it, but I think those two are in it together."

"We only have Rose Yerges' word about that," Haase said. "Other than that, what can we actually prove?"

"Maybe, nothing. But, it's time to have another talk with them and, this time, not in their comfortable living room. Get Wong and go bring them both in."

"What about the warrants?"

"I'll work on that." Austin sighed. "Crap. It would be so much easier if we had a body."

"What the hell do you think you're doing,

216

Daniel? Bringing me in here like I'm some kind of criminal," Joseph Larson shouted.

"I have a whole bunch of questions, Joseph, and I'm hoping you'll fill in the blanks for me."

"About what? I've already told you everything I know."

Austin pulled out a chair and sat down across from Joseph. He put a folder on the desk which separated them and sighed. "How long have we known each other, Joseph?"

Joseph shrugged. "I don't know. A long time, I guess." He grinned. "Hell, I knew you when you were just a little pup."

"That's right. And, that's why this is hard for me. You're an old friend of my dad's. And, I'll tell you right now, there are a lot of other things I'd rather be doing than sitting here questioning you."

"No shit. And, I'd rather be at work than be here talking to you. So, let's just get this over with. Now, what do you need to know?"

"What time did you leave work on Friday?"

Joseph stared at Austin for a moment, then, smiled. "Oh, that. You know I had the time wrong. When I got to work today, I checked my time card. I punched out around noon."

"And, you went right home, where you did some weeding before you went into the house. Is that correct?"

"That sounds right."

"So, you didn't drive to the Toyota dealer in Sun Prairie and have new tires put on your Highlander?"

Joseph looked shocked. "What? No, of course

217

not."

"There are new tires on your car, Joseph. Can you tell me when those were put on?"

"On Thursday. The day before Tillie went missing."

"The dealer says it was on Friday."

"Well, the dealer is wrong," Joseph stated, emphatically.

"I see. Okay, then. Let's move on, shall we? What did you do with your old tires?"

Joseph gave him a dirty look and sat back in his chair. "You know what, Daniel?"

"What?"

"I think I'd like to call a lawyer."

"That's your prerogative. But, if you do and you're done talking to me, I'll make sure you don't get any deal from the D.A."

"A deal for what? I'm telling you, I haven't done anything wrong," Joseph exclaimed.

"Then, why do you want an attorney?"

Joseph hesitated. "Forget it. I don't need one. Ask me whatever the hell you want."

Thirty

Sergeant Wong checked his watch, surprised that it was already two in the morning. He glanced through the open window of his squad car, checked out the Larson house once more, and yawned. He was tired and he wanted to go home and go to bed.

Just as he laid his head back on the headrest of his squad car, he noticed a car coming down a side street. He waited, holding his breath, hoping that this was Rosemary Larson finally coming home.

The car turned the corner, went a short distance, and pulled into the Larson's driveway. "Gotcha!" Wong exclaimed, started his car, and pulled in behind Rosemary. As the garage door started to open, he jumped out of his squad car. He walked over to the driver's side of the Buick and knocked on the window. "Rosemary Larson, turn off the ignition and get out of the car, please."

Sergeant Wong waited for her to comply with his instructions. He knocked on the window again. "Get out of the vehicle," he yelled again.

The car door opened and a voice called out, "I'm coming, for god's sake. Don't get your underwear all in a bundle, as my mother would say."

Wong suddenly realized that it wasn't Rosemary talking to him, but Stacy. "What the hell, Stacy," he said. "What are you doing here?"

"I brought Mom's car home. I thought Dad was going to pick it up earlier, but he never showed up."

"Do you know where your mother is?" he asked.

"Of course. She's in the house." She gave Wong

a confused look. "Isn't she?"

"What are you doing with her car?" Wong asked, ignoring Stacy's question.

Stacy stared at him. "Is mom okay? What's going on?"

"Why are you driving her car?" Wong asked again.

"I needed a car. Mine's in the garage and Mom said I could use hers. Dad was supposed to drive over with her tonight so she could pick it up, but they never showed up. So, I decided to bring it over."

"You do know it's after two in the morning, don't you?" Wong asked her.

"I couldn't sleep. All I can do is think about my grandmother. I was up, so I figured I'd go for a drive."

"And, how were you planning on getting home?" Wong inquired.

"I figured I'd call you and you'd come and get me and give me a ride," Stacy said, grinning.

"Like that would happen," Wong said, smiling.

"Seriously, I was going to walk. It's not that far, you know. Anyway. . ." She gave him a puzzled look. "What are you doing here at two in the morning?" Stacy asked.

"I was waiting for your mother to come home."

"What? You mean she isn't here?'

"As far as I know, she isn't in the house," Wong answered.

"What about Dad? He must be worried sick."

"Could you open the door?" Wong asked. "I'd like to check out the house."

"Oh, my god. Do you think something happened

220

to them?"

"Do you have a key?" he inquired.

"Wait a minute." Stacy reached into the front seat of the car and pulled out her purse. "I've got one," she told him and started walking towards the back door.

"Wait. I'll do it," Wong said, taking the key from her. He unlocked the door and let it swing open.

"Mom? Dad?" Stacy yelled, pushing Wong out of her way, as she entered the kitchen. She turned on the light and ran towards the living room.

Wait," Wong yelled, grabbing her arm.

Stacy pulled her arm out of his grasp. "I want to see if Mom and Dad are okay," she said angrily.

"Your dad isn't here, Stacy," Wong said. "He's being held at the station."

"What?" Stacy exclaimed, looking shocked. "What the hell is going on, Sergeant?"

"He hasn't been arrested yet. But things aren't looking good for him."

Stacy glared at him. "And, my mom? Are things not looking good for her either?"

"I'm gonna go check the rest of the house," Wong told Stacy. "I want you to stay here. Understand?"

Stacy looked at him, not sure what to do. "All right," she finally said. "I'll stay here."

A few minutes later Sergeant Wong walked back into the kitchen. "I need you to vacate the house. Don't go home, though. Just wait outside for now."

"Why?" She looked at Wong's face and knew something was wrong. "What about Mom? Is she

221

here?" Stacy asked.

"I'm so sorry, Stacy. I just found your mom in her bedroom. She's dead."

Wong took Stacy's arm and walked her to the back of the house. "Sit here," he told her, as he helped her into a lawn chair. "Can I get you anything?"

Stacy looked confused.

"Do you want some water or something?"

Stacy shook her head no, put her face in her hands, and wept.

"Are you sure she's dead?" Austin asked Wong, the minute he jumped out of his squad car.

"I'm sure. She's as cold as a fish." Wong told him.

"How long do you think?"

"No idea," Wong replied. "That's up to the coroner to decide."

"Right." Austin stood in the driveway, staring at the back door. "How'd you get in?"

"Stacy let me in. She was returning her mother's car."

"At two in the morning? That's kind of strange, isn't it?"

"I guess," Wong muttered. "I don't know." He waited for Austin to say something. "Are you going in?" he finally asked.

"Is she in the bedroom?"

"Yeah," Wong told him. "She's on the bed, fully dressed. Her hair is all combed and neat and it looks like she has a lot of makeup on."

Austin sighed. "Shit, Lee, you're thinking suicide, aren't you?"

"I don't know. My first instinct is to say yes, but you know we can't call it until the coroner sees her."

"Did you see a note anywhere?"

"No, but I didn't search the place, so I guess there could be one. My first instinct was to get Stacy out of there before she saw her mother."

"Does she know about her dad?" Austin asked.

"I mentioned it to her. She's a real wreck, Chief. I don't think she has any idea of what's going on with her parents."

"I'll still need to talk to her," Austin declared.

"Can it wait until morning? I'd like to take her home."

"I guess it can. Go ahead and give her a ride. It might be a good idea if you went in with her to make sure she's okay before you leave."

"You want me to come back here?" Wong asked him.

"No. Go on home and try to get a couple hours of sleep. We can finish up here."

"Thanks, but I doubt I'll get much rest." Wong started to walk away, then, turned back to Austin. "God, Dan, she looks just like she's sleeping," he said, a break in his voice. "She doesn't look dead at all."

The Columbia County Coroner declared that Rosemary Larson was indeed dead. He loaded her body into his van and drove away.

"It definitely looks like suicide," Austin declared.

"Well, those pill bottles were all empty, so I'm

guessing you're right," Sergeant Haase said.

"I guess I better go tell Joseph that his wife is dead."

"I guess," Haase said.

"I hate this, especially when it's someone you know," Austin stated.

Sergeant Haase glanced at him, aware that Austin was upset. "I'll do it," he said after a few moments. "I didn't know Rosemary like you did and I know Joseph and your dad are friends."

"It could probably wait until morning. We've still got a few hours of work here. I'll do it then."

"I'm going back to the station," Haase declared. "I'll go tell him."

"It should be me," Austin argued.

"Damn. Why would she do something like this? What could be so horrible that she had to swallow all those pills?

"I figure it has something to do with Tillie missing," Austin said. "She and Joseph have been lying since they first called us. Hopefully, Joseph will have some of the answers," Austin said.

"Well, I figure you are going to have to question him in a few hours, so let me go do this first. It will give him a few hours to let the news sink in."

"Thanks, Matt." Austin shook his head and sighed. "I love my job, you know. Until something like this happens and, then, I don't."

"I know. But not every day can be a good day."

Thirty-one

Joseph Larson looked like he had gone to hell and back. His face was red and puffy from crying, his clothes were wrinkled, and his hair looked like he'd been in a wind tunnel. When he saw Chief Austin approaching his cell, he jumped off the small, hard bed and walked the few feet to the door.

"How you holding up, Joseph," Austin asked, as he handed him a cup of coffee.

"How do you think?" Joseph yelled, ignoring the coffee. "My wife is dead and I'm locked up in this shit hole."

Austin looked Joseph in the eyes. "I can't begin to tell you how sorry I am about Rosemary," he said. "I truly mean that, Joseph."

"Yeah? Well, if you're so sorry, open this damn door and let me the hell out of here."

"Sorry, I can't do that. At least, not right now. I have a lot of questions and you're the only one with the answers. Your breakfast will be here in a few minutes. I'd like you to pull yourself together and eat something."

"I'm not hungry and I don't feel like talking to you."

"You need to eat," Austin said, still holding the coffee. "Do you want this?"

"Is it black?" Joseph asked.

"It's black and it's hot," Austin replied, handing him the cup again.

This time Joseph reached out and took the cup. "Thanks," he murmured.

"No problem," Austin replied.

"I want to see my dad," Joseph Junior demanded.

"Visiting hours are between two and four," Cynthia told him.

"Where's Chief Austin?" Junior asked, looking around the police station. "Is he here? I want to talk to him."

Sergeant Wong, who was standing within earshot of their conversation, walked over to Junior. "Is there something I can help you with?" he asked.

"I'd like to know why I can't see my father," Junior replied. "And, what's this visiting hour shit?"

Wong smiled. "That's just Cynthia messing with you."

Junior turned and stared at the clerk. "You think this is funny? My dad's locked up, my mother is dead, and my grandmother is missing," he yelled. "What the hell is wrong with you people?"

Cynthia, who looked like she was about to cry, stood up and ran towards the restroom.

"I'm sorry about that," Wong said. "Your dad is being interviewed right now, so you can't see him."

"Is he under arrest?" Junior asked.

"I'm not sure," Wong said. "You'd have to talk to Chief Austin about that."

"Well, then, let me talk to him."

"He's busy," Wong told him.

"This is bullshit," Junior shouted. He started walking towards the door, turned, and shot Wong a dirty look. "I'm coming back, Wong, and when I do, I'll

226

have an attorney with me."

"Fine. You can bring one, but so far your father hasn't asked for an attorney. And, you can't just bring him one until he does."

Junior clenched his fists, trying hard to hold his temper. "Yeah? Well, we'll see . . . Oh, screw you." He turned and walked out of the police station.

Cynthia walked into the room; her eyes red from crying. "I'm so sorry," she told Wong. "My dumb sense of humor is always getting me into trouble."

Chief Austin looked up from his notes and stared at Joseph, who had been moved from his jail cell to an interview room. "Again, I'm sorry about Rosemary."

Joseph glanced over at Austin and shrugged.

"I just got the blood workup report from the coroner," he told Joseph.

"That was fast," Joseph commented.

"Do you want to know what killed her?" Austin asked him.

Joseph shrugged. "I guess."

"She died from an overdose of prescription drugs. The coroner found Valium, Ambien, and Xanax in her system." He looked over at Joseph, who showed no reaction to the news. "That's a pretty lethal combination, Joseph. Where do you think she got all those drugs?"

"I guess they were left from when she had that anxiety attack a while back. I think it was last October, if I remember right."

"I'd like to go over some stuff that you might be

able to clear up for me. Do you think you're up to it?"

"Like what?" Joseph asked.

"Well, for starters, why didn't you call in and let us know that Tillie was missing on Thursday? Why did you wait until early Saturday morning?"

Joseph looked away.

"We might have found Tillie safe and sound if we had known early on that she had disappeared."

Joseph took a deep breath and let it out. "It wouldn't have made any difference."

"Why not?" Austin inquired.

"Because Tillie was already dead."

Austin sat back in his chair and stared at Joseph. "Really?" he exclaimed.

"But it was an accident. Rosemary didn't mean to do it, you know. It was that damn scooter." Joseph reached for a glass of water and took a long swallow.

"Go on," Austin prompted.

"Rosemary never saw Tillie when she pulled into the driveway. Tillie drove that damn scooter right in front of her car. Rosemary wasn't going that fast and, well. . ." Joseph took a deep breath and let it out. "Rosemary was on her phone. She was looking at her damn phone and never saw Tillie. She hit that scooter just right and Tillie went flying off. I guess she hit her head on the cement driveway and it killed her."

"So, if it was an accident, why didn't Rosemary call and report it?" Austin asked.

"She panicked. Everybody knew that she hated that scooter and that she couldn't tolerate Tillie riding all over town on it. She figured she'd be accused of doing it on purpose."

"And, it had nothing to do with the money?" Austin asked.

Joseph looked confused. "What money?"

"All that money that Lowell Dobson left her. If Tillie was out of the picture, then, Rosemary would be a rich woman. And, you'd be married to a very rich woman."

"That's the most preposterous thing I've ever heard," Joseph declared.

"It makes sense to me. So, what happened after Rosemary hit Tillie?"

"She called me and told me to come home as soon as I could. When I got home, Rosemary had put Red in the garage and had managed to get Tillie into a lawn chair in the backyard." Joseph smiled. "She looked like she was sleeping. Just taking in the afternoon sun and having a little nap." He closed his eyes. "I can still see her sitting there." He was quiet for a moment. "Anyway, when I got home and saw the mess we were in, we decided to cover it up."

"So, you dumped the scooter in the river, had new tires put on your car, and made Tillie disappear. Where is she, Joseph?"

Joseph looked away, not saying anything.

"Joseph, what did you do with Tillie?"

"Am I under arrest?"

Austin sat back in his chair, shaking his head. "What the hell do you think?" he finally said.

"I guess I am," Joseph replied.

Austin got up from the table and walked out of the room. "Wong?"

"Yes, Sir?"

"Would you go read Joseph Larson his rights?"

"I'd love to. Did you get a confession?" Wong asked.

"Yeah, I did. For him being an accessory to a murder."

"For killing Tillie?"

"For starters. I'm pretty sure he killed Lowell Dobson, too. But I'm still working on that."

Chief Austin poured himself a cup of coffee, took a sip, and put the cup down. "Can't anyone around here make a decent cup of coffee?" he said.

"What's that, Chief," Cynthia asked, looking up from her desk. "Do you want something?"

"Nothing. Just talking to myself," he replied, smiling. "I guess I'm getting old."

"That's a big 10-4," Cynthia said.

Austin laughed. "You didn't have to agree, you know," he said.

"I've read him his rights," Wong told Austin, as he walked back into the room.

"Did he lawyer up?" Austin asked.

"Nope."

"Good," Austin said and walked back into the room to continue his questioning.

"Joseph, I want you to be straight with me. The more you cooperate, the easier it's gonna go for you."

"What more do you want me to tell you?" Joseph asked Austin. "Rosemary accidentally hit and killed Tillie, we covered it up, and now Rosemary's dead. End of story." He put his face in his hands, starting to cry.

"I know it was wrong. I'm so sorry," he uttered softly.

Austin gave Joseph a moment to collect himself. "The only part of that story that I believe is that you covered it up."

Joseph looked surprised. "Everything I've told you is the truth. Why would I lie?"

"Here's what I think, Joseph. You knew that Tillie was the sole beneficiary of Lowell's estate. But, when Tillie said she was done with him, you were afraid that he would change his will. So, you saw an opportunity to kill him before that happened. You went back to his house after you and Stacy had put him to bed. You found the wrench in the garage and you killed him with it."

Joseph stared at him. "You have quite the imagination. That's a bunch of bullshit and you know it."

"Then, Tillie decides she's going to spend as much of that money as she can before she dies. She starts to buy scooters for her friends and she talks about buying an expensive retirement condo. Who knows what else she was planning to buy? But all you can see is that money disappearing before you can get your hands on it. So, what do you do? You and Rosemary plan how to get rid of her, knowing that you will inherit all that money."

Joseph shook his head. "You're one hundred percent wrong. You have no idea what you are talking about."

"Oh, I think I do. You killed that sweet old lady. I know it and I can prove it."

"Bullshit. You can't prove any of this garbage."

"You killed Lowell Dobson and you killed Tillie. And, now, Joseph, you will never see a penny of that money. My god, man! Why couldn't you wait? There's no way in a million years that Tillie could have spent all that money. Do you even have any idea how much money she came into when Lowell died?"

"Not really. Tillie never mentioned an amount. I figure it was a lot, though." He shrugged. "I guess at least two or three hundred thousand. I don't know for sure. Plus, there was the house and car and a bunch of other stuff."

"How about two or three million, you idiot? All you had to do was wait until she passed away and you would have been living on easy street. But you got greedy. You and Rosemary. So, you killed her, and for what? You'll probably spend the rest of your life in prison."

Joseph sat back in his chair and stared at Austin. "You're wrong, you know. I had nothing to do with Tillie's death. But it doesn't make any difference one way or the other now. Rosemary is gone. My life is over without her."

"You're right. Your life is over."

"After Tillie got that damn scooter, our lives changed. All Rosemary and she did was fight, fight, fight. Every day they were at each other throats, fighting about that damn scooter. But, that's it. There was no big plan to get rid of her and you're crazy if you think there was. And, I sure as hell didn't kill Lowell. And, if you think I did . . ." Joseph looked away. "Well, let's see you prove it," he murmured.

Chief Austin sighed. "I'm sorry to tell you this,

Joseph, but we found a note."

Joseph stared at him.

"Rosemary wrote a note before she died. It's a pretty long note, describing everything that happened to Lowell and to her mother. Basically, Joseph, she could no longer live with the guilt of knowing what you did to Lowell and what she did to her mother. She didn't accidentally hit Tillie on that scooter. It was planned, and you know it."

"You're lying. She didn't write a note. Rosemary would never do that to me," Joseph said softly.

"But, she did and I have it," Austin said. "Now, are you ready to tell us what you did with Tillie?"

Thirty-two

"I told you, I have no idea where Tillie is," Joseph stated emphatically. "If Rosemary wrote a note, like you said she did, I'm pretty sure she would have mentioned what she did with her."

Chief Austin wanted to beat the hell out of Joseph. He knew he couldn't touch the man, and he held his temper. But, one way or the other, he was going to make Joseph tell him where Tillie was. "Okay, Joseph, this is where we're at. I have you for killing Lowell Dobson and possibly killing Tillie. At the least, you were an accessory in her murder. I have you for hiding evidence and for lying to the police. I can throw in obstruction of justice and . . ."

"All right. I get it," Joseph yelled. "I'm going to jail for a long time."

"I could talk to the district attorney and see if he will make a deal if, and only if, you tell me right now where she's at."

"Before I do that, I want to see what kind of a deal you're talking about," Joseph said.

"That's fair." Austin reached for the pad of paper and a pen that was on the table. He pushed it over to Joseph. "Write it down."

"Write what down?" Joseph asked, looking confused.

"Everything. Then, I'm going to compare it to Rosemary's note and see if they agree. If they do, I'll recommend that the D.A. go easy on you."

Joseph hesitated. "I don't know. Maybe, I should talk to an attorney."

Austin reached across the table and took back the pad of paper and pen. "Fine. But, the deals off the table if you do." He pushed his chair back and started to stand up.

"Wait!" Joseph said. "Give me the paper. I'll write it out for you."

"I need you to write it all, Joseph. Don't let anything out."

"I know. Just go call the D.A. Okay?"

Two hours later, Joseph had completed his written confession. Chief Austin had talked to the D.A., who said he would consider a plea deal. Getting a confession and not having to go to trial would save the state a ton of money, he told Austin.

Chief Austin was at his desk reading Joseph's confession. "Damn!" he exclaimed.

Sergeant Haase glanced over at him. "What?"

"The son of a bitch didn't write down where Tillie is." Austin got up and walked to the back of the room, opened a door to the holding cell, and yelled, "Larson, you forgot something, didn't you?"

"Did you get a deal from the D.A.?"

"Where is she? You tell me right now or the deal is off."

"So, you did get a deal, then?"

"The D.A. has agreed to a lesser charge for Tillie's murder. Now, for the last time, what did you do with her?"

"Do you remember me telling you that I pulled weeds on the day she disappeared?"

"Of course."

"Well, I wasn't pulling weeds. It was more like I was digging a hole."

Austin stared at him. "You buried her in your yard?"

"We did. At first, we didn't know what to do with her, so we wrapped her in a sleeping bag and put her in the basement. Then, on Friday, I buried her down past those big bushes in my backyard. It's a pretty area with all the different types of flowers and rose bushes. I think she's probably happy there."

Austin turned and started to walk out of the room.

"Wait," Joseph yelled.

"What?"

"Don't you want me to write that down, too?"

"I need a couple of men and some shovels," Austin said, as he walked into the room

"What for?" Haase asked.

"We need to go dig up Tillie."

"He finally told?"

"He did," Austin replied. "She's buried in his backyard."

Haase shook his head. "That's just plain sick. How could he do that?"

"Who the hell knows," Austin shouted. "Obviously, the man isn't all there." He grabbed his hat off his desk and started out the door. "Cynthia," he said, getting her attention.

"Yes?" she replied.

"Call the coroner and put him on alert. Tell him we'll probably need him in the next hour or so."

Joseph had planted Tillie deep. The ground was rich and soft, which made for easy digging. They found her zipped up inside a sleeping bag, just as Joseph had said. The coroner had been called and they were waiting for him to arrive.

"How old was she?" Haase asked.

"Eighty-one, I think," Austin said.

"I really liked her. She was a real spitfire," Wong said. "I wonder how many times we went looking for her."

"Quite a few," Austin replied. "Once she got Red, though, that kind of came to an end."

"She had a lot of friends. The funeral will probably be packed," Haase commented.

Austin looked over towards the street and watched as a vehicle pulled up. "It looks like Dr. Allen is here," he said.

They watched as Dr. Allen got out of his vehicle and walked towards them.

"Where is she?" Dr. Allen asked.

"In back," Austin said.

Tillie was still in the sleeping bag, lying on the ground alongside the deep hole that had been her grave. Dr. Allen pulled down the zipper and opened the sleeping bag. "Shit!" he exclaimed.

"What is it?" Austin asked.

"Well, at first glance, I'd say she's got a lot of damage to her head."

Austin looked down at Tillie and took a deep breath. "That's a hell of a wound. Joseph Larson said

237

she fell off of her mobility scooter and hit her head on the sidewalk. Of course, that was after she was hit by a car."

"That makes a little more sense. If this is where her head met the driveway, she was probably knocked out immediately. I won't be surprised if I find that she had a concussion." The coroner looked up at Austin. "I need to take a look at her outside of the bag. Would you mind helping me lift her out?"

"Bag the sleeping bag for evidence," Austin told Sergeant Wong, as he and Dr. Allen gently laid the old woman on the grass.

Dr. Allen continued to examine her where she lay on the ground. Finally, he stood up and stretched.

"What do you think, Doc? Did the trauma to her head kill her?"

"Could be. But, right now, from what I'm looking at, I'd put my money on asphyxiation. I'll know more when I get her on the table, though."

"Just what are you saying?" Austin exclaimed.

"Look at her eyes."

"The whites of her eyes are all bloodshot," Austin declared.

"Exactly. This is what usually happens when a person dies of asphyxiation. It's just my opinion, but if I had to guess right now, I'd say she was buried alive."

Austin suddenly felt sick to his stomach. He turned and walked away from the Coroner, trying to pull himself together. He couldn't remember ever being this angry in his entire life. He took a few deep breaths and wiped away a tear.

Sergeant Haase walked up behind him. "Are you

okay, Chief?"

"No, I'm not okay," Austin exclaimed, not looking at him. "Just give me a minute."

A few hours later, Chief Austin was getting ready to call it a day and go home. He grabbed his hat and, as he started to leave, he heard the phone ring. He waited while Cynthia took the call, hoping it wasn't anything serious.

"Chief, it's for you," Cynthia called to him. "It's Dr. Allen."

Austin picked up the phone. "Austin here."

"Dan, I'm glad I caught you. I wanted to let you know that I finished the prelims. There's no doubt that she was alive when they buried her," the coroner told Austin. "She probably never woke up from the blow to her head. I can see why they thought she was dead."

"So, she suffocated?" Austin said.

"I'm afraid so, Daniel. I'm sorry."

"I hope they give the bastard the death penalty."

"Not in Wisconsin, my friend,"

"I know," Austin declared. "But, it's times like this that I wish Wisconsin had the death penalty. This man doesn't deserve to live."

"Well, he will never see the outside of a prison again, that's for sure. I understand he is waiving a jury trial."

"He is. He confessed to everything except killing Lowell Dobson. But Tillie's death is enough to send him away for life."

"I understand that his wife, Rosemary, left a suicide note. Didn't she mention anything about

Dobson?"

"There was never a note, Steve."

"Are you serious? You made it up?"

"I certainly did," Austin told him. "I told him that I was going to compare his confession to Rosemary's note and he better tell the same story or no deal."

"Well, I'll be damned."

"So, I kind of believe what he wrote down, you know. I really do think it was Rosemary that hit Red."

"Hit what?" Doctor Allen asked.

"Sorry. Hit the scooter. Tillie's scooter was named Red. Everyone in town called it that."

"Interesting."

"Do you want to know something else I just found out?" Austin asked.

"I'm all ears."

"All Tillie left her daughter was her house. The main beneficiaries of Tillie Weiner's estate were her three grandchildren and numerous charities."

"What?" Dr. Allen stated, obviously surprised. "I don't believe it."

"Well, believe it," Austin said. "When it came to Tillie, you just never knew what she would do. This town is going to miss her."

December, 2018

RED . . . . Susan L Pare'

Thirty-three

"The house sold," Stacy told her sister.

"Finally," Lynn said. "I never thought it would be on the market that long. Who bought it?"

"A family from Illinois named Gacy. It's a middle-aged man and his mother."

"Well, that's one last thing we have to worry about," Lynn said.

"Have you talked to Junior lately?" Stacy asked.

"I talked to him a few days ago. He's pretty much settled in his new house. He emailed me pictures of it. It's gorgeous," Lynn told her.

"It is. He sent me pictures, too. I'd love to live right on the beach. He sure didn't waste any time moving, did he?"

"Can you blame him? Simon and I are thinking of relocating, too."

"Noo! You can't leave," Lynn exclaimed. "First, Junior moves, and now you. I'll be stuck here all alone. What will I do without you?"

"Don't get excited. Simon and I are just talking right now. I think we'll give it some time before we make our final decision."

"Well, stay here. You know people have short memories. Before long, they'll stop gossiping about what happened. Anyway, have you . . ." Lynn looked away. "Never mind."

"No, I haven't seen him," Stacy said, knowing what her sister was about to say. "Have you?"

"I can't do it. I'm still so mad at him for what he did. I don't know if I'll ever get over it."

"Do you think mom was actually a part of it, Lynn? I mean, I just can't fathom that mom would ever do anything to hurt Grandma," Stacy commented.

"I guess we'll never know the whole truth. Dad is sticking to his story, saying that she was the one who hit her with her car."

"I know. But, my god, Lynn, they buried her alive."

"Dad said they were positive she was dead. Can you hold for a minute? I've got another call?" Lynn asked.

A moment later, Lynn was back on the phone with her sister. "I've got to go. I'll talk to you later."

"Who is it?" Stacy asked.

"No one."

Stacy laughed. "Is that what you're calling Sergeant Haase these days?"

"Who was that?" Chief Austin asked Sergeant Haase.

Haase put his phone in his pocket and glanced over at Austin. "No one."

Austin grinned. "You two seem to be going hot and heavy these days. Do I see wedding bells in the future?"

Haase's face turned red, as he looked away. "It's too soon to even think about that."

"You're not getting any younger, Matt, and if you want kids, you better. . ."

"Whoa!" Haase exclaimed. "Let's not put the cart before the horse."

"Just saying, is all." Austin opened his desk

drawer and pulled out a Snickers bar.

"It seems like you sure have a sweet tooth, lately," Haase commented.

"I know. All of a sudden, I want chocolate." He grinned. "Maybe, I'm pregnant."

Sergeant Haase laughed. "Seriously, though, when's the last time you got your blood sugar checked."

"It's been a while," he said, reaching for the phone.

"Chief Austin, Columbus Police Department," Austin answered. He listened to the caller for a few moments. "Thank you for letting me know." He hung up. "Well, I'll be damned," he declared.

"What?" Haase asked.

"They just found Joseph Larson dead in his cell."

"No shit," Haase exclaimed. "Was he murdered?"

"It looks like suicide. The warden said he left a note."

"Really? Anything interesting?"

"Nothing we didn't already know. It was mostly for his kids, asking them to forgive him and their mother for what they did," Austin told him. "And, he still emphatically denies having anything to do with Lowell Dobson's murder."

"Well, if he didn't do it, we'll probably never know who did," Sergeant Haase commented.

"You're probably right," Austin said with a sigh.

"

Epilogue

John stood in front of the graves, his head down, hands folded, and tried to pray. However, every time he got a few words out, he would start to laugh. Just like Tillie, he thought, as he looked at their headstone. The stone was made from Indian Red Granite, which was the closest to a real red the family could find. A scooter had been beautifully etched into the face of the stone. He liked it.

He read the inscriptions one more time. His name was on the right and her name was on the left. He smiled. Just the way we used to sleep, he thought. He looked at the year carved on the stone showing when he had died. He was surprised so much time had passed. It almost seems like yesterday when we said our goodbyes, he reflected.

"Do you like it?" she asked her husband.

He turned to her and took her hand. "I do like it. The grandkids did a great job."

"Are you ready to leave?"

He smiled at her. "I am."

"It's cold out, isn't it?" she asked him.

"It is."

"I can't feel it, you know."

"Either can I," he said.

"Then, how do you know it's cold?"

"Tillie, my love, it's snowing out."

She smiled. "It's so pretty." She squeezed her husband's hand. "Do you think they have scooters in heaven?" she asked him.

"I think there will be one there for you," he

replied.

"If there is, I'm hoping it's a red one," she told him. "I like red."

"I know." John looked to the skies and grinned. "Heaven is never going to be the same," he murmured.

About the Author

I was born in Idaho in 1939. My father's job demanded that we frequently move and, by the age of ten, I had lived in Idaho, Montana, Colorado, Michigan, and Wisconsin.

I am the proud mother of three wonderful sons and two fantastic grandsons. I have no plans to acquire another husband, as they are just too much work.

For most of my life, I worked as an accountant. Two years before I retired, I did a complete switch in careers and managed two Curves fitness facilities in Illinois. I retired in 2002 and moved to Branson, MO. In 2012, I moved to Indiana to be closer to my family and have resided in Highland since then.

I enjoy a good laugh and figure it's my sense of humor that keeps me going when times are tough. Reading has always been one of my passions and I still read a couple of books a week.

In 2014, I wrote my first book, *Blueberries and Bears and My Brother's Shoes*, a book about growing up in the forties and fifties. After I self-published it and gave it to friends and family to read, they encouraged me to get serious about my writing.

I never thought that, at the age of 76, I would become an author. I set a goal for myself to write at least ten books before I die. I've made the ten-plus and I'm pretty sure I have a lot more novels kicking around in this head of mine.

I certainly am enjoying my retirement knowing, when I get up each morning, I have something to look forward to. You can find out more about me and my books at www.susanlpare.com. Please visit me there, sign up to be on my readers' list, and feel free to send me your comments.

www.ingramcontent.com/pod-product-compliance
Lightning Source LLC
Chambersburg PA
CBHW071853220626
47052CB00002B/95